Sally never quite knew why she let him. She should have fought, should have screamed, should have sent him about his business the minute she felt his hand on her waist, but after the first gasp of indignation she couldn't. All she could do was wait, mesmerised, while he wrapped his arms round her and locked his mouth on hers.

What followed was worse. It wouldn't do her knee any good, and tomorrow she'd be nothing to him except maybe a scalp on his belt, but those were morning thoughts. Tonight, she was in his power just as she'd feared all along. And, just as she'd feared all along, she was going to enjoy it.

MAN OF TRUTH

BY

JESSICA MARCHANT

MILLS & BOON LIMITED
ETON HOUSE   18–24 PARADISE ROAD
RICHMOND   SURREY   TW9 1SR

First published in Great Britain 1991
by Mills & Boon Limited

© Jessica Marchant

Australian copyright 1991
Philippine copyright 1991
This edition 1991

ISBN 0 263 77238 1

Set in 10 on 11½ pt Linotron Times
01-9109-54364
Typeset in Great Britain by Centracet, Cambridge
Made and printed in Great Britain

CHAPTER ONE

'ANY more of that and I'll murder you!'

The words forced themselves into Sally's ear in a truly murderous hiss. And just to make sure she didn't do any more of that, whatever it was, he'd clamped a hand over her mouth, pinned her arms to the sides of her lime-green tracksuit, and pulled her backwards to him. Now she was pressed helpless against his body, which might have been made of warm steel.

Her light brown hair had fallen over her eyes. She peered through its swathes, trying to see into the moon-shot darkness under the trees. Where had he sprung from? Why was he so angry with her? What had she done?

And why was she wasting survival time on questions like this? Quite clearly he was mad. 'MANIAC MURDERS AGAIN,' the headlines would shriek. 'ADVERTISING EXECUTIVE FOUND DEAD IN SWISS FOREST. ENGLISH GIRL, 26, VANISHES IN ALPS. . .' This wouldn't do.

'Could you. . .?' She dragged in a long breath through her nose. 'Could we——?'

She broke off, struggling against panic. Even to her own ears she hadn't managed to make any sense, only wordless gurgles into that merciless, smothering hand.

'I don't want you here at all,' he whispered, biting his own words off sharp and clear. 'But I was going to let you pass and say nothing, till you started that damned caterwauling.'

So he really was mad. Her singing voice might not be good, but it wasn't bad enough for a death sentence.

She'd only been cheering herself up after the evening had grown too dark and the track too uneven to jog any more. Seeing that she had to walk, she'd been using her spare breath to sing 'All I want is a room somewhere', reminding herself that she *did* have a room, in a hotel which, thanks to her work, would soon be on the Kingfisher Travel brochures.

And now she might not live to see it. She turned her head sharply away from the thought, found his hand loosened from her mouth, and filled her lungs to scream.

And a lot of good that would do. The village twinkled peacefully on its plateau, quite unaware of the madman threatening murder above it. Nobody would hear but her attacker, and if he hadn't liked her singing a scream might be all he needed to go ahead and carry out his threat.

'Quiet, now!' Sure enough, his hand still hovered above her mouth, ready to slap down over any noise that displeased him. 'Are you lost?'

'It. . .' Sally gulped, breathed, and found a squeaky, up-and-down, would-be-casual croak. 'It depends what you mean by lost.'

'Keep your damned voice down!'

Oh, dear, he really did have a thing against noise. It must be the full moon making him worse. When she next spoke, she was careful to copy his own hissing whisper.

'I'll be quiet as a mouse the rest of the way.'

'You'd better be.' And then, incredibly, he let her go.

She couldn't believe it, stood frozen, dared not make the least movement. Then she ventured one step away from him. Another, and still no steely grip reached out to stop her. A third and she was clear of him, fear pumping the blood through her veins, body settling without her will into its low, streamlined sprint, legs shooting out ahead of her along the moonlit track. . .

Foot catching in a tree-root. Ribs thumping against the hard earth. Lungs straining for all the air they could get, which still wasn't enough.

'For Pete's sake!' He'd reached her already, a vast shadow folding itself down by her. 'Don't you know better,' he demanded, still in a whisper, 'than to try and run in these conditions?'

'Of. . .course,' she gasped, too stunned to remember that she shouldn't be arguing. 'I'm. . .not a. . .complete. . .fool!'

'Only a noisy one.' The shadow proffered a hand. 'Up you get.'

'Thank. . .you.' Sally rolled over and tried to scramble to her feet. 'I. . .don't need——'

She broke off, and fell back on her side. Something was badly wrong in one knee. Eyes hot with tears, head mazed with pain, she heard him cursing her anew.

'Hell and damnation, woman, is there no end to your idiocy?'

'P-please don't hurt me!' She hated herself for crying, but it had all been too much. 'I r-really d-didn't mean any h-harm.'

'Hurt you?' In the manner of madmen, he sounded honestly bewildered at the idea. 'Why should I? Come on, stop snivelling, and let's see the damage.'

And, before she could protest any further, he scooped her into his arms. Cradling her like a baby, he rose to his feet and set off along the track. So here she was, his prisoner again, and this time handicapped. Worse off than ever, though at least he was holding her gently this time.

Very gently indeed. Was it only shock and pain

making her drowsy like this? Or was there something else? Could it be the steady rhythm of his stride under the whitening moon, between the black, arching trees? Or the warm grip of his arms, one at her waist, the other so careful with her aching knee? Held against this strong chest she could almost be comfortable, almost feel ready to droop her head against his broad shoulder and let him do whatever he wanted. . .

She jerked away from him. 'Where are you taking me?'

'Would you mind not digging your fingers into my shoulder like that?' He didn't sound threatening any more, only quiet and soothing. 'On second thoughts, if it helps, feel free.'

'Free?' she echoed, defeated by his insane logic. 'Will I ever be that again?'

'Is it that bad?' He was taking the rough track at an easy lope, absorbing its ups and downs into his own springy muscles, giving her the evenest possible ride. 'Perhaps we should get you to a doctor.'

She felt her first glimmer of hope. Would a man about to commit murder take his victim to a doctor first? But, as she squinted up at the edges of his jaw and cheek and nose, the forehead blurred by what must be dark hair falling over it, her hope faded. Crazy people would do anything.

All the same, she couldn't let it go. 'A d-doctor?'

'Don't you think it might help?'

'There you go again!' She slumped back. 'Talking about help like any ordinary person!'

'I *am* an ordinary person.' Once more he sounded mildly, sanely surprised. 'And I'm trying to help you. Damned if I see what more I can do.'

'You could. . .you could have. . .you needn't have. . .'

'Save it,' he ordered tersely. 'I expect you'll make more sense in a minute.'

'*I'll* make more sense?'

She gave up, dropped back to the hardness of his shoulder, the smoothness of his shirt. The shirt was open at the neck, and from the base of his throat rose a scent of. . .pine? Fern? Musk? She couldn't tell, couldn't sort out the wildness of the dark, of leaf and earth and secret night creatures, from the wildness of this male being who had her at his mercy, who was carrying her heaven knew where, to do heaven knew what to her.

And she wouldn't be able to stop him. If she couldn't get away from him earlier, what could she do with one leg out of action? And all the time he was holding her so kindly, making it so easy for her to relax against him.

And, worse, setting her nerves in a turmoil she'd never known before. Was this how it felt when you were going to die? This sudden languor, the tingling in your spine where his arm held it, the prickling in your scalp where his breath lifted your hair? Was it knowing your life might end any minute which brightened and sharpened every sensation like this? Was that why you longed to fit your fingertips into the hollow at the base of that throat, to steal them under that shirt and find the further delights. . .

Sally pushed away from him again, trying to gather her wits. 'Are you going to rape me?'

'What?' He stopped dead. 'Do you honestly think——?'

'Only I'm a virgin,' she explained, gabbling a little to distract herself from the pain in her knee. 'I know I'm *old* to be a virgin, but there it is—I am one.'

'Heaven save us! Look—er—what's your name?'

'Sally.' She couldn't be doing this, introducing herself as if they'd just met at a party, but she was. 'Sally
Benedict.'

'Mine's. . .' He paused, apparently reluctant, then
started walking again and brought it out firmly. 'I'm
Kemp Whittaker.'

Nothing more, just the name, and she couldn't think
about that now. Things were changing, the trees thin-
ning from overhead, leaving the path naked to the
glaring moon and the rampaging stars. He was all black
and white against those stars—hair black and ragged,
nose a white jutting angle, eyes deep set and black and
mysterious above the bold white cheekbones.

And now the stars were blocked out by stone, a
stone gateway with a rounded top, and his feet were
ringing on cobbles. The castle? She hadn't been near
the castle, only seen it from below during their photo
session. It must be empty; a ruined lair for madmen at
full moon.

Whatever it was lay behind a massive, iron-bound
door. A door with a curved iron handle, and a modern
lock.

'Can you stand for a minute?' he asked.

'I could.' She responded unthinkingly to the rational
tone. 'On one leg.'

He lowered her feet to the cobbles. She stood half
balanced, glad against all reason that he was there to
hold her up, glad his hand stayed on her waist where
she needed it while he fished something from his
pocket.

Keys, it must have been. The door swung open and
he must have touched a switch. Yellow light spilled
from within, electric light, blessedly civilised even if it
did come from two naked bulbs close to the ceiling of
a low-arched, whitewashed corridor.

'I haven't decided what to do about this yet,' he chatted like any ordinary host. 'I thought I'd strip the walls down to the stones, but my architect says no.'

'Your. . .architect?' What was he doing with an architect, this forest elemental, this haunter of lonely places?

'Well, I pay him.' He was talking at normal volume now, a deep voice with husky overtones. 'But he calls the tune. This is a listed building, so you have to keep the——'

'Hang on!' Sally nearly fell against him, wondering how she could have overlooked this for so long. 'You're English!'

'Of course.' He hoisted her over the threshold, kicked the door shut, and started along the corridor. 'I told you.'

Sally heard the deep notes vibrating in his chest, and fought once more with that feeling of unreality. Why was that voice so familiar? And what was that name he'd given with such odd reluctance, yet as if it were bound to reassure her?

'I. . . I don't remember what you said you were called,' she said.

He squinted down at her in surprise, reminding her that, after all, he was mad. A local aristocrat, perhaps—the sad last of a crumbling line? But no, the name had been as English as the voice. Besides, the Swiss ran the longest-standing, best-organised democracy in Europe. They didn't have aristocrats.

She was still puzzling when he turned through a propped-open door and put her down on. . .

On a bed. A wooden single bed, big, plain, undisguised. Head pressed into its pillow, duvet crumpled under her, Sally closed her eyes and lay in fear, trying to prepare herself. Trying not to wonder what it was going to be like. . .

When nothing happened, she opened her eyes. Where had he gone? The only light came from the corridor, through the oblong of open doorway, but her eyes had adjusted, and he definitely wasn't in here. She shifted her weight, pushing the duvet from under her, and rose on one elbow to look for him.

The bed was in a corner, with papers strewn round it. Some of the papers lay half out of an office folder; others were scattered on the parquet. A bookcase ran along the wall from the bed, full of heavy volumes such as those a scholar, a doctor or a lawyer might use for reference. Its top was empty but for oddments—a video control, video tapes, a clipboard with more papers, a used tumbler whose exquisitely cut diamond pattern caught the thin light and sparkled, danced, changed colour. . .

'Here.'

'What?' Jolted back to herself, Sally accepted the clean tumbler and sniffed its contents. 'What is it?'

'Brandy. I keep it in the kitchen.'

'Then no, thank you.' She put it on the bookcase top.

He shrugged. 'Suit yourself. I brought it because you look as if you need it.'

'I need a clear head more.'

He clicked another switch, and the room filled with rosy light from the huge red shade of a huge wrought-iron lamp. Under the lamp, a huge armchair of brown leather faced a huge television set across a rug hand-worked in hugely bright colours. And there stood her captor, the giant of this giant's castle, immense and shadowy with his back to the light as he looked down at her.

'I do have coffee, if you can wait till I've boiled the kettle. I only keep instant up here.'

He didn't sound mad, any more than this seemed a madman's room. It was still a very strange room, a cell almost, not really small but with tiny windows let into white, immensely thick walls. Between two of the windows, a huge old table held about a million pounds' worth of electronic equipment.

'Come on!' He sounded impatient. 'Coffee, or not?'

'Not,' Sally answered at once and instinctively. If she ate or drank anything in this place, she might change into a frog, and be held in his thrall for all eternity.

'Right.' He approached the bed. 'Move over, then.'

She stayed where she was, braced to fight, eyes stretched so wide they smarted. 'Wh-what for?'

'So I can sit by you, and see what you've done to your knee,' he explained as if to a slow-witted child. 'That's why you're here, remember?'

'It's fine,' she snapped, suddenly as much irritated as scared.

'Oh, yes? You're ready to walk back down the hill, are you?'

'I'll get back somehow, if you'll let me go.'

'Of course I'll let you go, idiot!' He turned away from her in disgust, reached the armchair in one move, and dropped into it. 'What do you think I am—a kidnapper?'

'How do I know what you are?' she snapped.

'You know because I told you.' He sat back, the yellow light full on him. 'But if that's not enough, have a good look.'

'How would that help?' Sally struggled with a mythic terror. If you looked at wizards, they turned you to stone. 'How would it make you. . .?' She managed at last to raise her eyes to his, and caught her breath.

She *didn't* know him, she really didn't. Yet her first real sight of that face told her at once that these were the only possible features to go with that voice.

The mouth might be curving and sensual, but it was completely controlled. The jaw was lean, the eyes long, clear, anything at all but mad. The only wild thing about him was his hair, rioting all over his head, thrusting up at every angle, too full of life to lie flat— but the forehead under it was high, straight; the forehead of a thinker. Sally felt her mouth drop open.

'Satisfied?' His sigh might have been resignation.

'You're. . .you're Kemp Whittaker!'

'I told you.'

'It didn't. . . I didn't. . .you're so much bigger. . .'

'That's television. Stretches some, shrinks others.'

'The Truth man,' she murmured, trying to take it in. 'Are you here working on a new series?'

'I'm here to do my own thing. In peace and quiet.'

'Your own thing?' she spluttered, the hint of a rebuke turning her irritation to rage. 'So that's what you call it, jumping defenceless women!'

'Calm down,' he said. 'I didn't hurt you.'

'Oh, I see. So this is all right?' Sally pointed at her throbbing, swelling knee. 'Nothing to do with you?'

'You're the one who ran in the dark over rough ground.'

'And I didn't need to run, did I?'

The arm she was leaning on ached with tension, but she stayed up on it, facing him. His powerful denim-clad legs stretched right across the rug, almost to the television set. She flicked a furious glance from his leather boots to his narrow waist, and up to the wide sweep of his shoulders.

'You'd never need to be afraid.' She heard the tremor in her voice, and held it under control. 'But haven't you the least imagination? Haven't you ever thought what it's like to be a woman?' She leant forward, ignoring the pain in her knee, urgent with the need to convince him. 'A woman out alone in the dark?'

He stared at her, a small frown coming and going between his brows. 'Why were you, if it worries you so much?'

'It didn't, not with that beautiful sunset, and then the moon. I needed the exercise.'

She'd also needed to get away from her amorous married cameraman. She'd left him in the bar with his umpteenth whisky, shaking his head over what he called her morbid habits. Jogging, he'd said, could damage your health, and her temper rose anew at how right he'd been.

'Why am I explaining myself to you, anyway?' she asked crossly.

'It is private land,' Kemp Whittaker pointed out with an air of great forbearance.

'Yours? I see.' She remembered the signs on the diverted footpath. 'So it was you who put that fence up?'

'With good reason.'

'Well, I had good reason for climbing it.'

'To take the shorter path home?' He grinned sardonically. 'It didn't work, did it?'

'No. And, thanks to you, I'll never jog at night again.'

His frown returned, deeper. He shifted in his chair, the straight profile thoughtful, the eyebrows tilted in concentration.

Unable to hold up any longer on her tired arm, Sally flopped back. The pillow welcomed her; the bland shadows on the ceiling rested her tired eyes and her tired mind, an interlude of peace before she somehow had to get out of here and down to the hotel. At least, she realised with a growing sense of relief, she wasn't in fear of her life any more.

'Hell!' His expletive shot out like a bullet.

She jumped, her brief peace shattered. 'You should worry,' she retorted, up and fighting. 'I'm the one who's injured!'

'I wasn't. . .' He stopped, and rose. 'Let's at least make it easier for you to sit up.' He seized the giant-sized duvet and folded it as if it were a handkerchief. 'Forward!'

Somehow, when Kemp Whittaker gave an order, you obeyed. He put the folded duvet against the wall, and added the pillow.

'Now back.'

'I don't see. . .' She broke off, astonished at the snug way her back settled into the improvised cushion.

His job done, he returned to his chair. 'How's that knee?'

'Much better now I'm comfortable,' she admitted.

'Good.' He drew breath to speak, let it go, took another. 'Is it any use if I apologise?'

'You mean,' she gazed at him blankly, 'say you're sorry?'

'What the hell do you think I. . .?' He reined himself in. 'That's it. I'm sorry.'

'For jumping me?'

'For frightening you.'

Sally stared at him suspiciously. 'You really are?'

'Don't I look it?'

'You do now,' she admitted with some reluctance.

'Well, I am. You've made me see. . . I didn't re-alise. . .' He broke off. 'I'll do what I can to help.'

'There you go about helping!' she burst out as pain

darted through her knee. 'The damage is done; I'm out of action. How can you help that?'

'For a start, I can see you safely back.'

'Carrying me?'

She jerked upright at the thought of that weird journey through the dark forest to the unknown castle. He'd been a terrifying stranger then, and still she'd wanted to. . . Her mind veered from the thought, only to bump into a worse one.

She'd asked him if he meant to rape her. She'd confided in him that she was a virgin.

Was he remembering it too? Was that why he was suddenly so thoughtful?

It was. 'That's all part of what you've made me see,' he told her softly. 'And don't worry, I'll take you down in my car.'

'There's a road up here, then?' she babbled, hating her own foolishness.

'There is.' His voice was still soft, offering her a chance to recover. 'Look, I'm not pressing that brandy on you, but it's there if you want it.'

Sally looked at the crystal tumbler. It was so beautiful; liquid gold in a mesh of rainbow light. And so little of it.

'Whether you drink it or not, I'd be. . .' He broke off, finding it hard to get out what he wanted to say. 'I'd be grateful if you'd listen to me for a minute.'

'I haven't much choice, have I?' She slumped back, newly infuriated by her lameness, newly aware of how difficult it would make the rest of her schedule.

'Listen, Sally.' He'd remembered her name. 'I've. . .' He trailed off and re-started. 'I've frightened you, and made you hurt yourself. I'd. . .' he chose his words with care '. . .I'd appreciate a chance to explain.'

'And that has to be here?' she asked, suspicious once more. 'Why not at the hotel?'

'We could sit in the lounge, yes. But there'd be talk.'

She hadn't thought of that. Even here, in a quiet mountain village, he must be known. And in England he certainly was. Handsome Kemp Whittaker, photographed with one spectacular woman after another. Heartless Kemp Whittaker, jilting that pretty buyer after an entire Oxford Street store had heard him on the intercom, asking her to marry him. Hot-tempered Kemp Whittaker, who'd turned a garden hose on the Press last summer and soaked the T-shirt of the model who had happened to be with them.

'Who'd talk?' Sally pushed back her mid-length hair, aware of its boring mid-brown colour, the mid-blue-green of her eyes, the unsatisfactory, middling-to-shallow curves of her breasts and hips. 'I'm not the kind of woman you usually get mixed up with.'

'You think not?' His voice was suddenly harsh. 'Forget it. They mix me up with every kind of woman.'

She smothered a little stab of disappointment. She hadn't expected compliments, really not—she knew only too well how ordinary her own looks were. But it would have been nice if he'd shown just the least sign of interest. Just the tiniest hint that he didn't, after all, find her completely run-of-the-mill.

But I am, she reminded herself as she so often did. Or why hasn't Mark asked me out again?

'If I spend any time with you at the hotel,' Kemp Whittaker was continuing, 'the tabloids would be out here by noon tomorrow.'

'But you're taking me there anyway,' she objected. 'We're bound to be seen.'

'Not necessarily. I'm on decent terms with the locals,' he explained. 'They know I value my privacy.'

'You mean they won't talk?'

'Better than that. They let me use side-entrances.'

'So we sneak into the hotel, and our names aren't linked.' Irritated less with him than with that further, tiny stab of disappointment in herself, Sally swung her feet to the floor and managed not to wince. 'End of problem. Let's go.'

'You've forgotten the favour I asked.'

'Favour? Oh.' She reached for the tumbler and inhaled its heady fumes. 'You want to explain.'

'The reason I—er——' he paused, '—had to gag you.'

Sally recalled the terrifying hand over her mouth. 'You didn't like my singing.'

'Even you can't think it would be a treat listening to it?' he asked with a wry grin.

'It was a treat for me, doing it,' she retorted stoutly, 'and I wasn't disturbing——'

'You weren't what?' he interrupted on a note of renewed fury.

Sally gave him an apprehensive glance. This was exactly how he'd been in those first, horrible moments in the forest.

'You were like a blasted factory hooter.' The fury was still there, but smouldering. 'I was going to overlook the trespass, if you hadn't started that row.'

She took a sip of the brandy, barely enough to wet her lips, though it was half the contents of the glass. He certainly wasn't intending to get her drunk. The fiery, flowery smoothness gave strength to her tongue.

'I'd have been out of earshot in minutes.'

'By which time you could have scared her off the nest forever.' He thumped his chair in frustration. 'Maybe you have. I won't know till I've gone back and looked.'

'The nest?' Sally drained the brandy and put down her glass. 'You're talking about a bird?'

'Two birds. A nesting pair,' he brought it out as if to a drum-roll, 'of hawk owls.'

When she didn't react he stood up, took a book from the shelf, and opened it for her. She accepted it and the pictured owl glared up at her, yellow-eyed, white-faced, drab-striped as a city sparrow.

She stared in disbelief. All right, so he ran the television programme Truth, famous for its coverage of and sympathy with the earth's wild creatures. All right, so she'd trespassed on his land and ignored 'Keep Out' signs in five languages. But had he scared the living daylights out of her for this?

'Nesting,' he repeated, trying to impress it on her. 'They've never been known to breed in Switzerland before.'

'Oh, well, then,' she agreed with bitter sarcasm, 'that makes all the difference, doesn't it?'

'It does when. . .' He broke off and shrugged. 'If you won't see it, you won't.'

'And if you meant it when you said you'd get me out of here,' she retorted, bristling at the contempt in his tone, 'let's go.'

It was strange to be lifted by him again and not need to be afraid. His icy silence might be daunting, but at least she could be sure, as he carried her to the discreetly expensive car in the courtyard and drove her down the hill, that she was heading for her own room and bed. And if the prospect seemed a bit dismal, it was only because she was so tired after this long, peculiar day.

'If you have your key——' he parked in the shadowy square under the blossoming chestnut trees '—we can go in from here.'

'I can make it on my own.' Sally opened her door and struggled out on her good leg. 'I'll take the lift.'

'Key?' He was already at her side.

'I'll manage, honestly.' But she was glad to lean on him, and relieved when he lifted her again off her feet.

'Key?'

She gave up, and pulled it from her pocket. She was quite safe here. Quite safe, so why this sinking in her stomach? Why this weakness, this awareness of his strength? It made no sense, and yet that feeling of danger mounted as he carried her up the stairs. In her second-floor room, not even breathing hard, he left the door wide open, carried her to the bed, and set her gently on it. She could switch on this bedside lamp; quite safe.

'Go to sleep now.' He loomed over her. 'You look as if you need it.'

'Fine chance!' she retorted.

'It's hurting badly?' He sounded as if he really cared.

'It's fine as long as I stay still,' she admitted. 'But I've work to get on with.'

'We'll worry about that in the morning.'

'*I* will, you mean. You'll be with your wretched owls.'

'I'll be here seeing what I can do—for my sins.'

'You mean, for assaulting me.'

'All I did was stop your noise,' he growled, 'and I may have saved you from a lot worse. Nesting hawk owls can be dangerous.'

'So can heart attacks.'

'Somebody once lost an eye.'

'That's nothing to what I thought I was going to lose. . .'

Sally stopped, heat rushing to her cheeks with the renewed memory of her wretched, half-delirious prattle of virginity. He knew why she was blushing too: she saw it in the deep-set eyes before they half closed and veiled his thoughts.

Anger came to her rescue. 'You said you'd murder me.'

'It was only a. . .anybody would have. . . Hell!' He spun away, hands thrust deep in pockets. When he turned back, renewed irritation was clear in every line of his body, but his voice was low, controlled. 'I've already apologised for that, but I'll say it again. I'm sorry, I'm sorry, I'm sorry!'

'No need to shout!' Sally leant back on the bed-head, glad to feel superior. 'You're not acting sorry.'

'If you aren't the most maddening little. . .' He broke off, came to stand over her and dropped lightly to sit on the bed.

Sally never quite knew why she let him. She should have fought, should have screamed, should have sent him about his business the minute she felt his hands on her waist, but after the first gasp of indignation she couldn't. All she could do was wait, mesmerised, while he wrapped his arms round her and locked his mouth on hers.

What followed was worse. She shivered every time she later remembered how she had enjoyed it, enjoyed him, opened her lips to savour the hardness of his which tasted of pine and fern and musk. And when she raised her hands to push him away, they wouldn't. They wanted their share of him, wanted to steal between the buttons of his shirt and delight in the texture of his skin while his tongue raided and took possession of hers.

''Lo, Shally. Enjoying yourshelf?'

Sally recoiled in horror. 'Er—er—h-hello, H-H-Harry,' she stammered in an agony of embarrassment.

Of all the things to be doing with the door wide open! And of all people it had to be her randy photographer who saw them.

'Ish thish a private party?' He weaved about in the doorway with drunken good humour, ready to enter as soon as he stopped needing the wall to hold him up. 'Or can anybody join in?'

'Strictly private, mate.' Kemp reached the door as he spoke, pushed the fuddled Harry out of the way and closed it firmly.

When she saw him lock it, Sally gave up and waited for the worst. The best. The surrender she had so long delayed, to a mindless pleasure of the body she had so long denied.

It wouldn't do her knee any good, and tomorrow she'd be nothing to him except maybe a scalp on his belt, but those were morning thoughts. Tonight she was in his power, just as she'd feared all along. And, just as she'd feared all along, she was going to enjoy it.

CHAPTER TWO

'How could I ever have been such a fool?'

Turning yet again on her tumbled sheet, Sally dragged the duvet up to her ears, and tried yet again to sleep. And failed yet again, though her travel alarm showed a quarter to three.

At least he hadn't known how ready she'd been. Her tired mind offered the scrap of comfort yet again, and yet again had to reject it. How could he not know, when she'd returned his kiss like a besotted teenager?

Of course he'd known. He just hadn't been interested. That was why, once he'd shut out Harry, he'd stayed at the door. As far from her as he could get, he had surveyed her in the small glow of the bedside light with what could only have been distaste.

'I take it that was a friend of yours?'

'N-not exactly.' Sally had wanted to yell, but it came out hesitant and throaty. 'He's m-my ph-photographer.'

'I thought I knew the type.' The distaste was now open. 'I'll have to stay till he's out of the way.'

'Feel free.' Anger surged through her as she noted the smears of earth on her tracksuit where she'd fallen. 'What's a little intrusion on my night's rest, after what you've already done to me?'

'Er—yes.' Kemp glanced at his watch. 'Er—sorry about that. I—er—I don't always act very responsibly when I'm—er—when I'm irritated.'

Could he really be apologising for having kissed her? She wanted to hide under the bed. Or sink through a

24

hole in the ground and disappear forever. Or throw
something.

'So that's what you were.' Afraid of what he might
read in her face, she rubbed at the mud on the lime-
green fabric. 'Irritated.'

'With reason.' His voice had taken on that growling
note. 'You've been nothing but trouble since I first saw
you. Or should I say "heard you"?'

Sally jerked her head up to glare at him. 'What you
should say is "laid hands on me"!'

He looked down at his hands, then thrust them in his
pockets as if to keep them from further mischief. 'How
many times do I have to apologise for that?'

'Once would do, if you meant it.'

'I mean it all right. Look what you've got me into
now.' He indicated the door with a gesture of his head.
'I just hope your friend was too drunk to recognise
me.'

'Poor you!' she mocked, trying to ignore the acid
weight of humiliation in her stomach. 'He might spread
some nasty stories, mightn't he?'

'You'd suffer too. Or would you?' He gave her a
sharp glance. 'I hope you're not another damned
hack?'

She stared at him in incredulous rage. 'Are you
suggesting I've gone through all this for the sake of a
newspaper story?'

'Sally Benedict. I haven't heard of you.' He seemed
to try the name against a mental check-list. 'But maybe
that's the point. Maybe this is the assignment that's
going to make you.'

It was too much. Ignoring the pain in her damaged
knee, Sally hobbled to the dressing-table, opened her
chestnut-coloured briefcase, and took out one of her
lime-green business cards.

'I work for Limelight Public Relations.' She approached him, holding out the card.

'Not a lot better.' Hands firmly in his pockets, refusing to take it, Kemp glanced at it with increased distaste. 'For goodness' sake, get off your feet, woman!'

'What's the matter?' she spat at him. 'Afraid I'll needle you into kissing me again?'

That was when he'd spun round and unlocked the door. 'This isn't doing either of us any good.'

'It certainly isn't.' The humiliation within her had shifted, blended, turned to a bleakness she wasn't going to admit. 'Don't let me keep you.'

'See you in the morning.'

And that was it; he'd gone. Sally had hobbled through her bedtime chores, the pain in her knee almost welcome as a distraction from the turmoil in her mind. Within half an hour she'd been in bed, trying to sleep.

And failing. And still failing at half-past three, when she put her travel alarm on its face so she wouldn't see the night slipping away.

What on earth had possessed her? After hesitating all her life, had she really been willing to make love so quickly, so casually, when nobody had been able to persuade her before, not even Mark Walsh a month ago, though he'd tried so hard and made her want him so much?

Not even Kevin, back home in Newton. Kevin had been the first and, if she were honest, the only serious man in her life, but in the end they never had got engaged.

'How can we agree to share our lives,' he'd demanded, 'when we've never even shared a bed?'

It had seemed like good sense, yet somehow she

couldn't go through with it. Perhaps she'd been too young; perhaps something in Kevin left her unsatisfied. At any rate, it had all ended very naturally when she'd got the job with Limelight, and moved to London.

Working in public relations, you met a lot of attractive men. She soon grew used to the elegant clothes, carefully styled hair and name-dropping patter—in fact, she found it hard to tell one man from another. She couldn't take any of them seriously, until Mark Walsh had sauntered into her office and her life, and handed her the Kingfisher account.

When she had first seen him, she hadn't believed he was real.

To get a tan like that, he must spend his life on a sunbed, she'd thought. And his hair can't possibly be naturally that colour.

The hard green eyes under the startling Viking-gold fringe had slowly inspected her. She had moved uncomfortably at her desk, aware she was being assessed and graded according to some personal standard. Presently he had smiled as if she'd passed the test, and she'd melted in that smile as he'd told her the account was hers.

Sally had asked herself no more questions about Mark's looks and charm. She'd been too much under their spell. When he'd taken her out to dinner, she'd returned him signal for signal, glance for glance. Only at the end of the evening, when he'd given the taxi-driver his own address instead of hers, had she realised what she'd got herself into.

'No, thank you,' she'd said, knowing if she accepted his invitation for coffee she was lost. And then, 'No, really.' And finally, 'Please, Mark, *no*!' as she'd taken fire from his kisses.

He had coaxed, caressed, reasoned, raged. At last

he had called her a hateful name and stalked off, leaving her to make her own way home in the taxi.

She couldn't blame him, not for that nor for his coldness after. He'd accused her of leading him on, and she had. Now she could only work hard for Kingfisher, and wait till Mark forgave her for not being able to cross that line even with him.

And I was willing to cross it tonight with a stranger! She shook out her pillow for the umpteenth time. *A stranger I detest, who frightened me out of my wits. . .*

Frightened. Out of her wits. But of course! Her tired mind thankfully took the escape route it had stumbled on at last. She'd had a bad fright this evening, fallen and hurt herself, didn't know if she was coming or going.

'You kissed me because you were irritated, Kemp Whittaker.' She turned on her side with a sigh. 'Well, I kissed you because I was all shaken up.'

And on that thought she slept at last. She must have—the sun was streaming in.

Who had drawn the curtains? The tangled, lacy shadows of the window-box geraniums danced on the white walls. The light, though softened by the chestnut trees in the hotel garden and the lime tree in the village square, was still too bright to sleep through.

'Seems a shame to wake her, doesn't it?'

Sally frowned, and squeezed her eyes shut. Wasn't it bad enough suffering Kemp Whittaker while she was awake, without dreaming about him? And if he was going to shake her like this, how lucky that she'd brought this cotton nightdress, high to the throat, decently covering the shoulder he was grasping so firmly.

He went on shaking. 'I regret to disturb you, my dear, but I have other patients to visit.'

Sally's eyes flew open. Sure enough, it was a woman shaking her, silver-haired and wearing silver-framed glasses.

'Sally,' said Kemp Whittaker, 'this is Dr Elise Camuzzi. Elise, your patient, Sally Benedict.'

Sally struggled upright among her pillows to vent her indignation. But the words wouldn't come—neither her voice nor her mind were awake enough yet. While she opened and shut her mouth like a goldfish, Kemp Whittaker took the chair by the window, leaving this doctor what-was-she-called—this Dr Camuzzi—to push the duvet away from Sally's legs.

'You allow?'

But it was only a token request, murmured while she already bent to the injured knee. Sally winced as it was manipulated, but the hands were quick and careful, and soon done.

'A sprain, no more.' Dr Camuzzi stood upright, and picked up the black case which must have been on the floor beside her. 'You will need nothing from here.' She tapped the case. 'Only rest. About three days, a week maybe.'

'A week?' Sally's voice came back with a rush. 'I can't sit about in a Swiss hotel for a week!'

The other two exchanged glances.

'It's all right,' Kemp Whittaker said. 'I'll take over now.'

The doctor smiled, shook hands with each of them, and left.

'And who asked for a doctor anyway?' Sally demanded furiously as the door closed. 'It'll probably cost me the earth——'

'Not you.' He looked most unfairly content and refreshed this morning, a plaid shirt tucked into the same jeans or similar, the jeans tucked into the same boots. 'I'm paying.'

'But. . .' she knew how ungracious she sounded, but why should she thank him for meddling? '. . . I didn't need a doctor!'

'I did.' He stretched in the chair, a picture of healthy, outdoor manhood. 'I had to know the damage wasn't too serious.'

'Oh, great!' She flung herself round to face him. 'You've set your own mind at rest, and now I'm officially out of action for a week!'

'I can get you home, if it's important to you.'

'Would you? My plane's at eight. . .' Sally picked up her travel alarm and stopped in bewilderment. 'Surely it's later than half-past five?'

'It's ten to eleven.' He held up his watch for her to see.

'What a time for the damned battery to give out!' She threw the little clock to the mattress in despair. 'I should be nearly at work by now!'

'I saw your photographer leaving,' Kemp told her with disgusting cheerfulness, 'when I was down fetching rolls for breakfast.'

'He might have woken me!' But even as she said it, Sally remembered her problems with Harry. Besides, they'd both been quite convinced she'd be the first to wake by hours.

'He must have thought you'd gone ahead.' All unknowing, Kemp Whittaker confirmed her fears. 'He seemed in rather a rush. And hung over, of course.'

'Do you think he'd have made it?'

'For eight, you said? Yes, he'd have made that all right.'

'Great!' This time she almost wailed it. 'So the pictures get back, but I don't.'

He studied her for a moment, that small frown coming and going between his brows. His great shaggy head was framed against the green-dappled window, but even so she could tell the colour of his eyes in the bright morning light. They were a keen blue-grey, the kind of eyes that noted everything and filed it as information for the busy mind to work on.

'There are other planes,' he offered at last. 'I could book for you, and drive you to the airport.'

'Would you? Please?' Sally flung back the duvet and swung her feet to the floor. 'You can ring the airport from here. . .'

She suppressed a gasp of pain as she stood up. Kemp was at her side at once, but she spread her hands, holding him off.

'I'll manage,' she told him curtly, and tried not to notice that wild scent which wasn't pine or fern or musk, but which was so much him.

He stayed watchful as she lurched to the bathroom. Her knee had stiffened in the night, and now it buckled and threw her sideways every time she tried to put her weight on it.

'You get on with finding out about planes.' She grabbed the bathroom door and held on. 'I'm fine.'

'You're not.' The blue-grey eyes wouldn't be deceived. 'It's still hurting, isn't it?'

'I'll manage.'

But she wouldn't. She knew it as soon as she sat down in the bathroom. Once the weight was off her injured knee the pain retreated, and left her free to imagine what it would be like hobbling on to a plane. Hobbling off it in London. Hobbling to the office. Lurching into the boardroom for the Kingfisher meeting with Mark. . .

It's no use, she admitted to herself. I might just as well stay here till it's better.

When she emerged from the bathroom in her dressing-gown, Kemp Whittaker was waiting by the phone. Sally returned his enquiring look with a slight shake of her head, forcing herself not to show her pain, and lurched thankfully back to bed while he stood by ready to help.

'I'm glad you've thought better of it,' he told her when she was sitting with her feet up once more. 'You might have done yourself long-term damage.'

'You reckon I haven't?'

She thought of the Kingfisher job, now almost complete. She'd made nearly all the decisions, planned and noted where to buy the advertising, kept Harry sober while he took the inspired, enchanting pictures only he could produce. All that remained was the enjoyable part, choosing which of them to use, putting the brochure together in its final form, ordering the space in various magazines, and at last, after all her hard work, attending the meeting to show off the results.

'My career,' she announced glumly, 'may never recover.'

'I'm sorry about that.' Kemp spoke very simply, as if he meant it. 'But it may look better when you've eaten.'

She shook her hair back in a fury. 'What difference is a bit of food going to make?'

'You'll see.' He took up the phone again. 'It's high time you had breakfast.'

Listening to him ordering it in vigorous German, she hated him more than ever. This was all his fault. Thanks to him, her own plans were wrecked and her glamorous new assistant was going to get just the chance she'd been waiting for.

Ever since her arrival a month ago, Tara Spence had been trying to build her own empire. Now she could step in to give the Kingfisher deal its final touches, and look every bit as good as her absent senior who had done all the spadework. No, she'd look better, far better, than an executive who was fool enough to hurt herself and miss a plane and get held up in Switzerland.

'It's on its way.' Kemp Whittaker hung up the phone with satisfaction. 'You'll enjoy it.'

'You want to bet?'

But she did. The scents of fresh bread and good coffee set her appetite going the moment the uniformed maid opened the door. Once the bed-tray was arranged on its short legs over her lap, she could hardly wait to start. The soft-boiled egg was the creamiest she had ever tasted, the thin slices of gruyère strong yet delicately flavoured, the black cherry jam a perfection of fruitiness. As for the coffee and the crackling rolls, they vanished almost before she knew she'd had them.

While she ate, Kemp talked to her about the castle. He had only recently bought it, and was gradually adapting it as his home.

'I'm surprised they let you have it,' she commented through a mouthful of roll and butter.

'It wasn't easy,' he agreed. 'I had to make all sorts of promises about preserving the integrity of the building.'

'Would you like some coffee?' Reluctantly hospitable, Sally upended the pot. 'We could always send for more.'

'Thanks, I had all I wanted at breakfast.' He took the tray out of her way. 'Now, doesn't the world seem a better place?'

'Why should it?' she asked, though it did.

'I'll give you one reason. My hawk owls are still there.'

'And I'm supposed to clap my hands about that?' She stared at him in outrage. 'My schedule's up the spout, I may lose the account I most value, I'm in pain. . .'

'Are you?' He put the tray on the dressing-table and turned in genuine concern. 'Would a cold compress help?'

She brushed the offer aside, a little guilty at having exaggerated the odd twinge from her knee. 'That's the least of my worries. Now, if you could save the Kingfisher account for me. . .'

'Kingfisher.' He dropped to the chair, sorting through another of those mental check-lists. 'Aren't they the people who package those fancy hunting holidays?'

'Expensive and exclusive hunting holidays,' she corrected. 'That's them. Or that's him, rather—it's entirely Mark's baby.'

'That'll be Mark Walsh?'

'You know him? Wait a minute—of course you do.' She remembered the Kingfisher launching, long before the account had passed to her. 'You had him on your programme, didn't you?'

He nodded. 'He claims to run the greenest travel firm in Europe.'

'That's more than just a claim.' Stung by the distance-keeping tone, she strove to convince him. 'He'll be selling only six places here at the Hotel Engeldorf, for each of the three autumn hunting weeks.'

'I doubt if he could get licences for more.'

'He couldn't,' she agreed. 'The laws are very strict here.'

'So he tried? He hasn't changed, then.' The blue-grey eyes chilled. 'He still acts like God's gift to nature, while getting away with anything he can.'

'That's not fair!' she flashed, infuriated by the phrase 'God's gift'. 'If you're only going to undermine my faith in my client——'

'So you're doing business with Mark Walsh?' He looked her over, then rolled his eyes to heaven. 'Oh, babe!'

Sally recoiled, outraged. 'What a hideous expression!'

'The meaning's not very pretty either.' Kemp fixed her with a new, uncomfortable stare. 'How long have you had this account?'

'Two months, though I don't see it's any of your——'

'Two months?' The strong-arched eyebrows rose in ironic disbelief. 'Didn't you tell me last night you were a virgin?'

'What? How. . .how *dare* you bring that up?' She felt the colour flooding her cheeks. 'When it was your violence that made me say it!'

'So it was,' he retorted, equally angered. 'I believe at the time I was violently helping you recover from hurting yourself.'

'You know perfectly well what I mean! It's not the kind of thing a woman talks about.'

'Especially when she's working for Mark Walsh.'

Sally crushed down the memory of that marvellous evening with Mark, and its miserable ending. After all, he *had* taken no for an answer—eventually. She drew herself up, as grand as it was possible to be with legs horizontal and pain stabbing at one knee.

'I don't know what you're suggesting——'

'I'm not suggesting, lady—I'm telling. If you're

mixed up with that guy, watch out.' Kemp stood, momentarily blocking out the pink-blossoming chestnut trees. 'There aren't any hunting laws to protect women.'

'Don't I know it!' she called after him as he made for the door. 'Having been jumped in the forest!'

'Will you ever let me forget that?' Hand on the doorknob, he swung round to face her. 'Haven't I done what I can to make up for it?'

'You've brought a doctor, to clear your conscience.'

'And now I'm off to book your room for a week, to clear my conscience some more.' He opened the door. 'Believe me, the sooner you're out of here, the clearer my conscience will be.'

'It can't be too soon for me!'

But he'd already closed the door.

What manners! Carrying on the argument in her head, Sally hobbled to the dressing-table for her briefcase. She wasn't looking forward to calling the office and explaining her absence, but it had to be done, and the sooner the better. At least she'd be able to show she had this end of the job all wrapped up.

'Oh, poor you!' Tara cooed into the phone a few minutes later. 'Is it hurting badly?'

'I'll live.' Sally brushed the honeyed sympathy aside, wondering why she was always so brief and blunt when talking to her junior. 'Has Harry got in touch yet?'

'No, but——'

'You may have to go after him. His address is in the book.' He was most likely at his favourite lunchtime pub by now, but Tara could do her own research on that.

She seemed quite confident she could. 'I'll get him to develop the pictures, and I'll explain your problems to Mark,' she told Sally.

'I'm sure you will.'

Sally could imagine the explanation, though she'd rather not. Mark, who hadn't met Tara yet, was sure to enjoy that guinea-gold hair and those sparkling, tailored good looks, she realised as she wound up the call.

To take her mind off it she hobbled to the stand that held her little suitcase. Not that it helped much. What you packed for a two-night, one-day visit was quite different from what you'd put in if you knew you were staying a week. It would just have to be her jeans again, and the blue cotton shirt she'd worn for yesterday's expeditions round the village. Now, if only she'd put in more shirts, and left out this flame-red, backless, almost topless scrap of a silk dress which had given Harry such ideas in the bar last night. . .

By the time she'd finished showering, her good leg was aching from having had to take all her weight. But at least she was clean, clothed, and in her right mind when the phone buzzed.

'Hi, sweetie.'

Sally closed her eyes, took a deep breath, and returned the familiar greeting as briskly as she could. 'Hello, Mark.'

'You poor little thing! What have you done to yourself?'

'It's nothing. Only a matter of a week's rest.'

'Good, good.'

A short pause. In the glass-walled office high over London, he might be tapping his gold pen against that perpetual-motion toy, as he did when concentrating. Or running perfectly manicured fingers through that Viking-gold hair, which would quickly fall back into the same perfect lines as before.

'So you're staying on at the Hotel Engeldorf?' he asked.

'Well—er—yes, I suppose I am.'

The lilting voice hardened and took an edge. 'Have you any idea what they charge, sweetie?'

'I can afford it.' Anxious to assure him it wouldn't go on the Kingfisher bill, Sally rushed on, 'The doctor says——'

'Doctor? You can afford that too?'

'I don't need to. Kemp Whittaker's paying.'

Another pause. This time, somehow, it focused full on her.

'*Who* did you say?' He spoke from a sudden tension, as if sitting bolt upright.

'Kemp Whittaker,' she repeated, confused by his new urgency. 'You know, the Truth man.'

'Twenty-four hours in the back of beyond,' Mark sounded almost respectful, 'and you've got a TV personality paying your bills?'

'He isn't. . . I wouldn't. . .' Horrified, Sally struggled to correct the sordid false impression she'd created. 'It isn't like that at all. He just happens to own land round here, and I——'

'You mean he's living near Engeldorf?'

'Well, in it, I suppose—at the castle. But he's hateful, Mark.' She remembered that they'd met. 'Didn't you find him hateful?'

'As if that made any difference! Honestly, Sal, sometimes I wonder about you!'

'I. . . I suppose it doesn't,' she murmured, shamed by the rebuke.

'At the castle,' he marvelled. 'And paying your bills.'

'Only for the doctor. It was. . . Oh, dear!' She despaired of straightening him out. 'It was his fault I fell.'

'So he owes you one?'

'I wouldn't have put it like that.'

'He owes you one,' Mark repeated, decisive as ever. 'So you shouldn't find it too hard to get his backing.'

'B-backing?' Sally floundered. 'Whatever would I——?'

'For the brochure. The Truth man!' he exclaimed, unable to believe his luck. 'A famous naturalist and conservationist, in the very area I'm trying to sell.'

'But, Mark, he'd never. . .' She trailed off, choked by Kemp Whittaker's bruising scorn for Kingfisher, Limelight, the whole world she'd been a part of for five years.

'Never what—co-operate? Then make him,' Mark instructed coolly. 'That's what I pay you for, sweetie.'

'I. . . I suppose it is,' she faltered.

'Kemp Whittaker, the Truth man, at his home in Engeldorf Castle.' The light voice warmed and caught fire. 'All we need is his permission, and a picture.'

'*All*?' Sally repeated helplessly. 'Have you any idea how he feels about publicity?'

'I should have—I got on his programme. And that,' a hint of iron crept into the smooth tone, 'was before I had you to help.'

Sally felt a sudden chill. Mark had been with Sullivan Brooke in those days—she'd often wondered why he had left them. Could he be giving her a clue?

'Come on, Sal!' His voice softened to its low, coaxing note. 'You can do it. And I'd be so pleased.'

'Would you?' she asked, torn.

'Wouldn't I just! It'd make all the difference.'

Gone was the chill of recent weeks. This was Mark at his most charming, as he'd been when he first gave her the account. Spellbound as ever, Sally found herself promising that she would try.

Only when she hung up did the enormity of what she had promised return to her. Was she to start asking favours of Kemp Whittaker, with whom she'd barely exchanged a civil word since their first meeting? If meeting it could be called, that incident which was the cause of all her troubles. How would she begin—take an interest in his wretched owls, perhaps? He'd see through that at once, especially if she apologised for having disturbed them.

The idea brought her up with a start. Everything had happened so fast it had never occurred to her that, after all, he did have reason to be annoyed. If he'd been wrong to frighten her—well, so had she been to trepass.

'And I can see my singing might drive them away,' she ruefully admitted to herself. 'It may not be tuneful, but it certainly is loud!'

She remembered how, last night, she had gradually made him see what he'd done to her. He'd taken it in, understood, and yes, angry though he still was about the disturbance, had shown he understood by apologising.

And he meant it, she realised. He's horribly rude, and he does have a filthy temper, but, as he said, he's doing all he can to make up.

That made it a lot easier.

'Come in,' she answered the knock five minutes later. 'Is it Mr Whittaker?'

He entered, and stood just inside the door. 'You'd better call me Kemp.'

Arranged once more on the bed with her feet up, Sally stared at him in surprise. Why the sudden invitation to use his first name? And why did he seem so awkward, embarrassed almost, never once glancing at her as he strolled to the chair and dropped into it?

Well, she had a new job to do, and had better get on with it. While he was in this mood, it might be easier. She drew a deep breath.

'I'm sorry I made such a row near your owls,' she said.

'What?' He looked at her now all right, arched brows drawn together.

'And I'm glad they're still at the nest,' she rushed on, realising with surprise that she meant it.

However, Kemp wasn't so easily convinced. 'You didn't sound glad when I told you.'

'I've—er—I've had time to think about it while you were away.' Which was, after all, nothing but the truth.

'Time to come round a hundred and eighty degrees, and suddenly get interested in wildlife?' The blue-grey gaze didn't waver. 'Time to stop fussing about your schedule, your job——?'

'*Fussing*?' she echoed, furious. 'It's all right your carrying on about a couple of birds——'

'A minute ago you were sorry you'd disturbed them.'

'Well. . .well, I am,' she asserted, glaring at him.

'You could have fooled me.' He leant back in triumph. 'You're not acting sorry.'

'Oh, you. . .you. . .'

Sally broke off, wrestling with her temper as she recognised her own taunt of last night. These same words had angered him so much that he'd. . . Her mind veered off that one, and sought for ways of putting her case.

'My job means a lot to me, and I'm worried about it,' she managed at last with difficult restraint. 'I don't think it's kind of you to call that fussing.'

To her surprise, he seemed impressed. The silence stretched out, and turned into one of those long, considering moments she was beginning to recognise, when he was thinking something over.

'You're right,' he said at last. 'I shouldn't have talked of fussing. And—er—listen.' He shifted his feet, looked out of the window, glanced at his watch—could the embarrassment be back? 'I've—er—I've bad news.'

'Don't tell me!' Embarrassed herself by the task she had been set, Sally tried to joke. 'I'm to be deported for having a harmful effect on Swiss wildlife?'

'Not that bad.' He grinned, relaxing. 'But the hotel's fully booked for the rest of the week. They need your room.'

'Is that all?' Recalling that she was paying her own bills, she felt little more than relief. 'Well, it's a nuisance, of course, but surely there's somewhere else?'

'Er—well. . .that's why I've been so long,' he explained.

'You mean there isn't?'

'The Webers are away visiting, and the Herdis are full.'

'Local families?'

'Farmers, who let rooms.' Kemp met her eyes ruefully. 'Nobody else does.'

Sally stared out of the window, grasping the extent of the problem. They were deceptively urban, these perfectly shaped chestnut trees. The smart hotel, the neat village square, the comfortable houses all made you forget how high Engeldorf lay above the valley. Beyond it were only isolated farms and miles of forest, and, beyond those, the mountains.

'There must be *somewhere*,' she protested at last.

'I could ring one of the hotels down in the valley,' he began reluctantly.

Was she to have all the pain and bother of a move, only to end up helpless in a place where she wasn't even known?

'I suppose you'd better,' she agreed, equally reluctant.

'Hear me out. I only wanted you to know the possibilities.' He raised one boot and stared very hard at its scuffed toe. 'But the best thing would be for you to rest at my place.'

'The castle?' she asked in surprise. 'But you're still sort of camping there, aren't you? I thought you only had the one room in use.'

'I have, and that's where I'll be living,' he assured her hastily. 'Where you'd be is in my farmhouse, just below the castle.'

She saw at once how that would help to keep gossip to a minimum. 'Why—er—thank you,' she said hesitantly. She ought to be jumping at the offer. It was exactly the chance she needed to get on with him a little better, and be able to ask the favour Mark wanted. Why was she so reluctant, so glad to find a practical objection to the plan? 'But—er—how do I look after myself?'

'I'll get Frau Huber from the village to help. The most respectable lady you can imagine.'

And another way of silencing gossip.

'So you wouldn't need to come near me?'

Sally found it an unwelcome thought, and not only because of Mark's plans. In fact, not at all because of those—the very idea of them made her shiver. Or something did.

'I wouldn't need to come,' Kemp agreed, 'but I would.' The blue-grey eyes met hers at last, patently serious and sincere. 'The least I can do is help you get well again. That much I owe you.'

CHAPTER THREE

'WATCH this!'

Sally spread her arms wide in a theatrical gesture, and rose on tiptoe. Bare feet revelling in the lush spring grass, she crossed the garden's small, precious patch of level ground, and finished with a ballet-class curtsy to show off the strength of the once-painful knee.

'Careful!' Kemp stayed on the other side of the little gate. 'We don't want a relapse.'

'There won't be one.' She twirled back to the garden chair to collect the book she had been reading. 'It's as good as new.'

'I'm glad. Even if. . .' He broke off, glanced down at the gate, and opened it as though the small task needed all his attention.

'Even if what?' Sally picked up the book, and danced through the opening to stand on tiptoe before him. 'Even if I do caper around like a fool?'

'If that's capering, I like it.' He closed the gate with great care, and gestured at the stone steps to the house. 'Shouldn't we go in? Frau Huber hates to keep good food waiting.'

'It's salad, and Frau Huber's. . .' she faltered as the keen eyes met hers at last '. . .g-gone h-home.'

This, she realised with a shock, was what she had been playing for since he had arrived just now. He'd spent the last three days not looking at her. Today, without understanding what she was doing, she'd been determined to make him.

Now she had succeeded, she wasn't sure she could

handle it. Something unexpected smouldered in the blue-grey depths that was banked down and hidden before she could retreat from it. She retreated just the same, lowering her own gaze to her bookmark as she fiddled it into her book.

'I s-said I'd c-clear up today.' She heard her own stammering, and willed her tongue to behave. 'To celebrate being mobile again.'

'You've a strange idea of celebrating.' Kemp put a hand below her elbow, barely touching, just enough to move her up the steps ahead of him. 'I'd have thought a drink on the veranda was a better idea.'

'It's ready.' Glad to change the subject, she led him to the narrow, wood-railed gallery with its spectacular views. '*Citron pressé*, the way you like it at midday.'

She slid along the veranda's single bench. Before her on the table, a gilt tray held a rainbow-cut jug clinking with ice-cubes, and two matching glasses whose diamond patterns sparkled with reflected green and scarlet from the geraniums along the railings. On its plateau below, the village had quietened for midday, and the hot light hung gauzy over the mountains on the horizon.

'May I?' murmured Kemp.

It was a token question—the short bench was the only place to sit. He folded his great length beside her, and that wild, unidentifiable scent mingled with the peppery green of the geraniums.

Sally hurriedly grasped the jug. She knew he was sitting as far from her as possible, but that was still too close.

'That's it, then.' He dumped his field-glasses between them on the bench. 'There's nothing to stop you going home.'

Home. The idea brought her up with a start. Home

meant not the white house in Newton, but the cramped little Kingston flat where she went after the day's work.

But work—yes, she must certainly think about returning to that. Having recovered in three days instead of the threatened week, she might still be in time to wrest the Kingfisher job away from Tara.

Only, she thought, it doesn't seem nearly so urgent now.

Not after three days here. Three days of idling, reading, eating Frau Huber's simple meals, waiting for Kemp to drop in to see how she was.

When had she started liking him? *Really* liking, seeing the honesty and kindness that lay behind his bad temper? She couldn't tell, but it was bound up with realising how lucky she was to have been invited here at all. This old farmhouse had been his first hideaway, his real home.

And then he had bought the castle, Sally smiled to herself, because the romantic in him couldn't resist it.

The first two days, he'd visited from there in the evenings. Yesterday and today, he'd made it at lunchtime too. She would have liked to think this was because he enjoyed her company as she enjoyed his, but she didn't know. He'd never said, though they both talked a lot. He spoke with enthusiasm of his student days at the Royal Veterinary College, and of the university lecturing post from which he had gradually drifted into television.

'And I'm still not sure I did the right thing,' he had confessed.

'Oh, but *Truth* is a marvellous programme,' she'd protested.

'It's too much of a damned circus sometimes. Like so much of life.'

He hadn't wanted to enlarge on that. Gradually,

though, she had learnt that his father had been a diplomat, and his childhood one of nannies and boarding schools and holiday times spent in one capital or another.

'But that sounds so exciting!' she had told him.

'Well, it wasn't.'

And he'd encouraged her to talk about her own home. Speaking of her parents, her pets, her young brother Simon who might fail his 'A' levels if he didn't come in from the open air and study, Sally had grown quite nostalgic for them all. She must visit them soon.

'Your brother sounds like my kind of guy,' Kemp had commented, and in his darkroom up at the castle had developed an extra print of his photo of the hawk owls' eggs, especially for Simon.

She'd have to pack it in the little suitcase which had seemed so inadequate three days ago. As it turned out, those jeans and shirts had been all she'd needed here.

'I can see how I mended so quickly.' She poured lemonade carefully, not spilling a drop. 'It's been a whole different way of life.'

And now it was to end. In the thrill of being strong again, she'd forgotten that. And she still hadn't been able to bring herself to speak of the Kingfisher brochure, let alone ask Kemp's consent to their using his name and photo.

She couldn't. Whatever he might feel he owed her, he had paid it in full by inviting her into this haven of privacy where the world never came. So she hadn't mentioned Kingfisher, or anything else about her job, all the time she'd been here. Other things had proved so much more interesting.

'I'll miss the hatching out,' she said with real regret.

'Not necessarily.' Kemp knew at once that she meant the owl chicks, due to peck their way out of the eggs at

any moment. 'Had you forgotten it's Saturday
tomorrow?'

'Is it? I'd lost count.' Sally replaced the jug with the
utmost care.

'A rotten day to travel.' His eyes were full on her.
'Why don't you stay over the weekend?'

'I'd. . .' she paused, controlling the tremor in her
voice '. . .I'd like that very much.'

She pushed his full glass along the grained, silvery
wood. He accepted it in silence, and before she could
withdraw she found her fingers trapped under his.

She caught her breath, frightened by the sensations
that swept through her. She'd never felt anything like
this before. Caught to the unyielding surface of the
glass, she welcomed its icy cut edges, a boundary to
the engulfing fire of that hand which covered hers.

But, once she had met the blue-grey eyes, she
couldn't refuse their demand. When he loosed her
convulsive grip on the glass, she didn't resist. When he
raised her chilled, burning fingers to his lips, she could
only let them rest there, marvelling at the hardness and
heat and gentleness of his mouth. He moved his lips to
her palm, the cushion of her thumb, the pulse of her
inner wrist. She shivered, and he cradled her hand in
both of his.

'See those?' He indicated the field-glasses, still on
the bench between their bodies. 'A lot of good they've
done me!'

'Y-you m-mean,' her own voice came to her small
and muffled, 'they're not working?'

'They're fine for looking through.' Kemp laid her
hand on one of his, ran his fingers over the back of it,
and let them circle her wrist. 'They haven't stopped me
touching you, have they?'

'D-did you mean them to?'

'That's why I put them there.'

'But why, Kemp?' She dared to meet his eyes. 'You haven't wanted to look at me either. Why not?'

'Looking—touching.' The unsettling blue-grey gaze stayed full on her. 'I suppose I'd better come clean. Ever since we met, I've been wanting to. . .' He paused, searching for another way of conveying his feelings. 'It was bad enough that I kissed you back there in the hotel, at a time when you were already upset.'

This, Sally recalled, had been exactly her own explanation for the way she'd responded to him. Now she wondered anew about it, and quietened her breathing, and struggled to overcome the languor that crept through her from that warmly circled wrist.

'I suppose,' she suggested, 'it was an odd situation for both of us.'

'I shouldn't have given in to it.' Kemp sighed, set her hand gently on the table, and downed the icy lemonade in one gulp. 'I was a bit stirred up myself, though. Holding you in the forest was like catching a young hare.'

'A hare?' She looked down miserably at her rejected hand. 'Something brown and small and insignificant.'

'Something wild and soft, with secrets you can learn if you're patient. Which I wasn't.'

'You have been since.' Driven by the new chill, the loneliness of that hand no longer joined to his, she let it trace the glittering pattern on her glass with one finger. 'I've. . . I've liked being here, Kemp.'

'It's been great. But. . .' He sat up with an air of resolution. 'Listen, Sally. You don't like me to refer to what you told me in the forest.'

She bit her lip, knowing exactly what he meant.

'But—well, it's there, isn't it?' he went on. 'You're

not a girl who makes love as easily as cleaning her teeth.'

She winced. 'And I suppose you know lots who do?'

'I did once, yes. But we're talking about you, and how I've been wanting you quite. . .' He broke off, and pushed away his glass as if fearing to harm it. 'Quite violently. Ever since I first touched you. Now do you see what I mean?'

She nodded, amazed at this world of feeling she hadn't understood or suspected. Now she knew, it was easier to make a confession of her own in return.

'That night when you kissed me, you could have gone on——' she told him.

'Couldn't I just!'

A little scared by the forceful, heartfelt interruption, she persisted, 'I. . . I didn't mean just *you*.'

'No, you're telling me you'd have. . .welcomed me. Do you think I don't know that?'

Had it been so obvious? Had she seemed so easy? Sally lowered her head and put her ice-chilled hands to her hot face. She didn't see Kemp reach out; only felt the backs of his strong fingers raising her chin. Gently, persistently, they forced it up, made her drop her hands, made her keep her head high.

'Don't be ashamed.' The deep voice comforted even though he kept her facing him, refusing escape. 'It was my fault.'

Then his eyes burnt into hers, and the quality of his touch changed. His fingers turned, caressed the skin of her throat, traced a tingling, delightful track to the open neck of her shirt, and came to rest on its first closed button. She gave a little frightened gasp and he quickly withdrew, spreading his hand wide and stiff on the table before him.

'And this is how you feel when I don't. . .seduce

you.' He spoke with an effort, the words torn from somewhere deep within. 'Now, just imagine if I had.'

Sally kept absolutely still, afraid of what that spread, powerful hand could do to her. What it could make her want. This time he hadn't even kissed her, yet she didn't want him to stop. Her body was already preparing itself for him, ready to surrender to those hands, those lips, in secret places no man had ever known, places she had hardly been aware of herself until now.

'Come on, Sally,' he urged. 'Face it. If we'd made love that night, if we made love now the way I. . .' He swallowed, and went on gruffly, 'If we did that, and asked the questions afterwards, you wouldn't like the answers.'

'W-wouldn't I?'

'For you it's got to be the right man, or you'll end up hating yourself. And him.'

She nodded, admitting it. She couldn't trust her voice. If she tried to speak, nothing would hold back the question clamouring on her tongue, and she didn't think she could bear the clear, obvious answer.

But she knew it. Pride forced her to say it before he could.

'And the right man isn't you.'

It came out flat, dreary, but definite. In the intoxication of the past few minutes, she'd forgotten who and what Kemp was: a man known to millions, sought out wherever he went, seen with beautiful women by the score. How could she hope to compete? Heavy with her own disappointment, she heard his voice from a great distance.

'I'm not.'

He was agreeing with her, she realised. And if she needed more proof, he was already visibly calmer.

'How could you be,' she asked, misery washed away by a healing anger, 'with your track record?'

His calm turned to chill. 'I see you read the tabloids. But aren't you a little out of date?'

'Some stories run and run,' she retorted, stung by his contemptuous tone. 'And Jacqui Lane's always on the telly.'

Kemp made a small noise, almost a hiss. Sally glanced round, and saw his profile sealed and stubborn under the unruly dark hair. When he spoke again it was through clenched teeth.

'I'd rather you didn't mention her, if you don't mind.'

So he'd been hurt too. That period years back, when Jacqui Lane had spoken so often and so publicly about her broken heart, he hadn't said a word. The way he refused all contact with the Press, and the famous bad temper when reporters did catch up with him, had become news items in themselves.

The whole affair had been news. First the unknown, elegant brunette had become his more and more frequent companion. Then the papers had started calling her Jacqui, and published interviews with her. Finally, one midsummer afternoon, sales customers all over the store where Jacqui worked had been treated, via the intercom, to every word of their quarrel about Kemp's going away.

'Right, so what's it to be?' he'd shouted at last, and offered the choice which became a catch-phrase that summer.

'Marriage, or Madagascar?' Sally murmured, more to herself than to him.

Kemp shot to his feet so quickly that she jumped. When she had steadied the wildly rocking jug and glasses, she raised startled eyes to where he stood, huge and dark and menacing against the white of the distant mountains.

'I've asked you politely,' he rapped out. 'Now I'm telling you. I won't be reminded of that business!'

'I'm s-sorry——'

'Or any of that part of my life. Damn it, woman——'

'I do have a name,' she interrupted, depressed by this further evidence of how little she meant to him.

'You also have a mind, so hear me out.' He thrust his hands in his pockets, and turned to brood across the valley. 'Have you any idea how long I've lived quietly, away from the headlines?'

Sally shook her head, though once more he wasn't looking at her. His eyes were fixed on the distance, far away in time as well as in place.

'Five years!' He drew it out, angrily marvelling that it wasn't long enough. 'As against two years when I was an idiot, a—a *celebrity*.' He spat the word in disgust. 'Dazzled by having people run after me, having women. . .' He broke off, and whirled to stare down at her. 'I learnt. Five years ago I learnt, and you talk as if nothing's changed!'

'I do not!' she flared. 'It's you who's been doing all the talking!'

'Such as about my track record?'

'Well. . .' Sally bit her lip, aware of how she'd thrown that at him to cover her own mortification '. . . I've said I'm sorry, haven't I?'

'And where have I heard that before?'

To her surprise, the anger left him as quickly as it had come. She could almost see it draining away, his muscles relaxing, as he moved to lean against the doorway into the house.

'We do rub each other up the wrong way, you and I, don't we?'

Now it was her turn to avert her eyes. She looked down at her hand on the table and kept it tensely still, determined not to remind him of the other effect he could have on her if he chose.

'I shouldn't be loading my hang-ups on to you, anyway,' Kemp's voice continued over her head. 'You're no worse than the rest of the public.'

'Thanks!' She blinked across the valley to hide the humiliation of being so dismissed. 'Just one of the millions, that's me!'

'I didn't mean. . . Oh, well.' He shrugged, and stood aside to invite her through the door ahead of him 'Shall we eat?'

Sally struggled to her feet, and went ahead of him through the door as he indicated. It was like passing a fascinating, dangerous animal. One whose presence made you shiver, and you tried not to shrink away because that would show its power over you, but neither did you risk going any nearer it than you must.

The cool, wood-scented spaces of the house offered a welcome relief from the dazzling sunshine. After all, she reminded herself, she loved it here, and he was her host. But for him she'd never have had the chance to enjoy this simple, glorious room with its bookshelves, its old-fashioned piano, its tiled stove and its scatter of bright rugs on the shining parquet.

The great table in the corner was set with the meal they were to share. The windows around it stood open, because she so much enjoyed leaning out and staring. On this side you could see right down to the tiny main roads and houses of the distant valley; on that side to the mountains which changed with every light.

'I nearly forgot.' Kemp drew a long white envelope

from his pocket. 'When I was in the village just now, the hotel gave me this for you.'

Sally took it with a resigned glance at the London postmark. The real world had to catch up with her some time, and now it was about to wrench her from this dreamy interlude. She remembered her unfulfilled mission, her failure even to approach the subject of asking Kemp for his help on the brochure, and dread settled in her stomach as she opened the letter.

It was worse than she had feared. Mark had used the vividly headed Kingfisher paper, but had been too annoyed, or in too much of a hurry, to dictate his message to a secretary. His black flourishes covered the page with very few words, but every one counted.

Where the hell are you? I can't get any sense out of the hotel. I'd be forgetting the whole thing by now if I didn't have an idea you're holed up nicely in a place where you could be very useful to us.

Obscurely ashamed, Sally folded it quickly out of sight. And yet she couldn't run away from it. Mark wasn't the kind of person who would accept sick leave as an excuse for anything. If you wanted to stay with a firm like Kingfisher, it was no use asking to be left alone till you felt better.

Besides, she *did* feel better. It was time to start work again. She straightened her shoulders, put the letter by her plate, and served herself salad from the wooden bowl.

'I need to call London.' She accepted the crusty bread Kemp had cut. 'I'll go down to the village this afternoon.'

'Whatever for?' Lifting the cover from the tray of smoked meat, he indicated the phone in its ledge

between their L-shaped corner benches. 'Do you think
that's not working?'

'I—I can't land you with that sort of expense.'

'What sort?' He laughed, and passed her the tray. 'I
ring London all the time. And Australia, Tokyo, Los
Angeles. Have you enough there?'

'Yes, thanks.' She returned the tray without enthusiasm. 'That's kind of you. I'll give him time to get
in from lunch.'

'Whenever you want.' Kemp filled his own plate.
'I'm going back to the castle in a minute, to write up
my notes.'

So she'd be alone to make her call. Kemp would be
up in that forest lair, putting into the word processor
the notes he had jotted in his dense, square script
which was so full of movement and yet so easy to read.
Down here, she would be able to sit at this table and
say exactly what suited her.

The idea brought no comfort. Whatever she and
Mark had to say to each other, it couldn't help but
bring a jarring note into this orderly quiet. The worlds
of Limelight and Kingfisher just didn't belong here,
even if she were able to tell Mark what he wanted to
hear.

And she must, she realised in near-panic, have
something to tell. She must be able to show she'd at
least been trying for Kemp's name on the brochure.

She sought for a way to raise the subject. 'If he isn't
there, could I leave your number for him to ring back?'
she asked.

'That depends.' He stopped eating to give her a
considering stare. 'Who exactly are we on about?'

Sally nodded at the envelope. 'It's Mark.'

'Mark Walsh?' Kemp frowned, shrugged, and went
on eating. 'You really want to talk to him?'

She stiffened at the contemptuous surprise. 'Can I remind you that this is my job?'

'I hadn't forgotten. Limelight, however,' he ate doggedly, 'happens to be a thing I don't want.'

It was so exactly as she had expected, she felt hardly any disappointment. 'So I mustn't give him your number?'

'Not only that. You mustn't tell him I live here.'

'I——' Sally put down her knife and fork, and forced herself to be honest '—I'm afraid I already have done.'

'*What*?' Kemp clattered his own cutlery to his empty plate. 'When? Why? What the hell did you think you were up to?'

She huddled up on the bench, the storm every bit as bad as she'd feared. 'It sort of slipped out. I didn't mean to. . .'

'Are you sure?' He slid from his side of the corner-bench with a lithe movement, and stood up. 'You didn't just happen to mention it as a way of helping your wretched campaign?'

'No, Kemp, I swear. . .'

But she had to stop. How could she swear any such thing, when she'd just been looking for a way to ask him exactly that? She stared up at him, in the wrong and worried anew by his massive height, which reduced the solid table to a mere toy.

'I. . . I really didn't mention you on purpose.' This at least was the absolute, simple truth. 'As for the campaign, I've hardly even thought about it while I've been here.'

'I believe you.' Kemp nodded. 'These last three days, you've been growing more human by the minute.'

'I see. Let me get this right.' Sally eased out of her own side of the table, stood up, and glared. 'Being human is idling round in a dream, and not worrying about real life?'

'It all depends what you mean by real life.' He turned, and made his way to the door.

She followed, infuriated. 'My job is what I mean! The way I earn my keep.'

'And there we have it,' he threw over his shoulder. 'You earn your keep helping pests like Mark Walsh to make worse pests of themselves!'

He left the room, and she kept after him. She must look like—what had he called her?—a hare, stalking a shaggy wolf, but she didn't care. Hares too had their rights.

'You really can be *detestable*!' she announced in the hall. 'Don't stop to ask yourself any questions, will you?'

'Like what?' Kemp paused at the front door.

'Like maybe some of the things I promote are useful.'

'I'm glad to hear it.'

He didn't sound glad, he sounded disbelieving. Sally cast about in her mind for an example—Lantern Soap? Silk Mascara? She gave it up, and found another way to attack.

'And supposing Mark Walsh isn't as bad as you think?'

'Supposing pigs fly? And you talk about real life!' He pulled out his car keys, balanced them on his palm, and went on slowly and clearly, as if she were deaf or stupid or both. 'Mark Walsh is every bit as bad as anybody could think.'

'Even if that were true,' she shot out, determined not to let him get away with the last word, 'you might remember he's my job.'

'Exactly.' He had reached the stone steps up to the

road, but paused on the first. 'I'd better say it in words of one syllable. Your job's a pain, and so are you when you're doing it.'

'O-oh, you. . .' Sally felt a flush which rose right to her hairline. 'What about you, the way you talk about it?'

Kemp made a swatting movement and swung up to the Range Rover on its tiny piece of flat ground. Another moment and he was gone.

Though she had had the last word, that final gesture had been more powerful than any words. It had dismissed her, flattened her and her affairs like a fly, left her to get on with this nonsense she considered her job while he got on with his.

She wished she didn't feel so guilty.

How was I to know, she continued the argument in her mind, that he'd be so morbidly keen to keep this place quiet?

But it wouldn't do. Not in the sunlit calm of this traditional, wood-built farmhouse he had renovated so lovingly. Clearing the table in the beautiful living-room, washing up in the discreetly luxurious kitchen, tidying herself in the equally luxurious downstairs bathroom, Sally knew he deserved to be left in peace here, in the home he had worked so hard to create.

Which didn't make it any easier talking to Mark. When he first came on the line he sounded cool, comfortable, languorous almost, but his satisfaction soon dispersed.

'You've been three days with Kemp Whittaker, of all people,' he exclaimed in disbelief, 'and he isn't eating out of your hand?'

If she hadn't been so depressed, Sally could have laughed. 'Kemp would never,' she stated with complete conviction, 'eat out of anybody's hand.'

'Or not yours, anyway.' He would be pushing at the
weights on that perpetual-motion toy; you could almost
hear them clinking. Or perhaps the clinking had got
into his voice. 'Honestly, Sal, you missed out somewhere on your basic training as a woman!'

She gripped the phone, trying to match his lightness.
'And what do you suggest I do about that?'

'Ask Tara,' he suggested with a chuckle. 'She could
teach you a thing or two.'

'Tara,' Sally reminded him with a sinking heart, 'is
my trainee. I'm supposed to be teaching *her*.'

'Which only goes to show. Though I don't say she
can't learn.' That cool, languorous note was back in his
voice. 'She can. Most enjoyably.'

So they'd been getting to know each other. Sally
pushed away the insistent, disturbing pictures the idea
conjured up, and held to the fact that this was her job.
She must keep talking, keep her voice professional.

'I'm glad she's giving you satisfaction.'

'Oh, she's doing that all right.'

'Then perhaps,' Sally took a deep breath, and prepared for the worst, 'you'd like her to take over the
account?'

'Did I say that?' His tone changed at once. 'Don't be
so hasty, Sal! You're still the one who can get to Kemp
Whittaker.'

'Not on this, I can't.' She hated admitting it, but it
might as well be settled now as later. 'He's never going
to help with this promotion.'

'Don't be so sure. You just try being nice to him,
and we'll see what happens.'

'Mark,' she began in exasperation, 'if you had any
idea——'

'I'll be in touch.' And he hung up.

Sally returned to the garden, but her peace was

shattered. She'd have rung the airport to book her flight, but she wasn't sure when she was leaving. Kemp had asked her to stay till Sunday, but did he still want that, now he knew how she'd. . .? *Given him away* was how it came into her mind, but she resisted.

'I didn't mean you any harm,' she found herself arguing with him as if he were there. 'And I didn't profit from it in any way.'

But hadn't she? Her mind plodded reluctantly, relentlessly through the facts. If she lost the Kingfisher account, she might well lose her job, especially with Tara so willing and able to take it on. But, for the moment, she still had it. Still had the chance to make a success of it, and perhaps persuade Kemp. . .

'It's no use, he never would.'

The argument went round and round in her head. It was still going late in the afternoon, when she looked up from her unread book in the living-room and heard with dread the note of the Range Rover being manoeuvred into its little parking space. Its door banged, and Kemp's feet sounded quick and light on the stone steps. Was he still angry with her? Angrier?

When he walked in, she had the confused feeling that sparks might be shooting out of him. They were not, however, of anger.

'It's happened!' He raised his hands in the air, showering the room with his sparks of victory. 'The first chick's out!'

'Why, Kemp, that's marvellous!' She was on her feet before she knew it. 'What's it like?'

'All skin and beak—the ugliest little brute you ever saw.' He covered the short distance between them, and flung those victorious arms round her. 'Like a little Tyrannosaurus.'

'But that's a dinosaur!' Her own arms fitted so

comfortably round his neck, they might have belonged there.

'Birds, dinosaurs. . .' He drew her close, turned her face up to his. 'Some people think. . .'

She was sure the kiss surprised him as much as it did her. She really had been thinking about dinosaurs, and owl chicks, and then suddenly she wasn't thinking at all, only feeling, hungering, longing. His lips took hers like fire, like bread, like wine, all she needed and all she had ever wanted. She must have more, must be consumed and fed and made glad, must surge to him as his hands pressed at her back, must open her body as she opened her lips. . .

She pulled away, panting and breathless. 'I. . . I'm sorry,' she whispered.

'So am I.' Slowly, reluctantly, as if losing a part of himself, Kemp put her to one side. 'You're hard on a man, Sally.'

She stared at the woven rug. 'I don't mean to be.'

'That's why.' He flung himself on the couch. 'Do you think you could do this to me if you were just any little tease?'

Sally flinched. That word had been part, the repeatable part, of the name Mark had called her. But these deep eyes saw at once how it affected her.

'I said you weren't, didn't I? What you are,' he added ruefully, 'is a kind of unexploded bomb.'

Repelled by the military image, she started to protest. 'I'd never hurt anybody. . .'

'We could both end up shattered,' he insisted, his mouth a decisive line. 'Thank heaven I'm not spending the nights here!'

'Do you want me to go?' It seemed only decent to make the offer, though it left her suddenly empty and desolate.

He frowned—was it in surprise? 'But of course you're going. On Sunday evening, as we agreed.'

'I. . . I meant earlier than that. Tomorrow morning.'

Kemp stared at her, the frown deepening. 'If you want to, then of course you must.'

'I didn't say *I* wanted to; weren't you listening?' Sally's own aggressive tone caught her unawares. She paused, and went on more quietly, 'An. . .an unexploded bomb's something to get rid of, isn't it?'

His eyes narrowed, considered, met hers again. At last he settled back, spread his arms along the back of the couch, and thrust his legs out in front of him. The pose was easy, indolent, yet the angle of his head stayed watchful.

'Put it like this,' he said. 'I'll take the risk if you will.'

CHAPTER FOUR

SALLY put down the silvered glass phial, sniffed at her wrist, and wrinkled her nose in dismay. When had this perfume turned so heavy and cloying?

'It must be the mountain air,' she told her reflection, and tilted her head quickly away from it.

Like the perfume, her dress was more striking than she had realised. Surely the red hadn't always been so harsh? And how could she ever have felt comfortable in these bootlace straps, this swooping neckline? Yet when she'd first worn it, at the Silk launching, hadn't she been rather pleased with it? More than pleased: flattered by the glances it had attracted, and by the way Mark's eyes had glittered as they'd lingered on her exposed flesh.

I was hoping he'd take me home. She fastened the three strands of gold and amber beads at her throat. *Why does it all feel as if it happened to someone else?*

She had already known, at that time, what being alone with Mark Walsh would lead to. Had she really wanted to risk repeating it? And in this dress, which gave her no more protection than—she glanced down at the floating silk, which stirred with the softest rise and fall of her breathing—than the petals of a poppy.

I must have been mad, she decided.

But she had to face it. She'd chosen the dress on purpose, with Mark in mind. She'd meant to tempt him into giving her another chance, making love to her again. And if he had. . .

But he hadn't. She shook out the lacy, fringed wool

triangle of her wrap, and draped it round her shoulders. Ah, that's better! she thought.

Well covered, she could once more face herself in the glass. The shawl was too hot for this May evening, but she could bear it until dark. After that the lamplight would tone her down, and she'd feel less. . . No, she must stop thinking words like 'brash'—they'd only worry her. She forced her mind back to this party for the birthday of Dr Elise.

'Her fiftieth,' Kemp had explained. 'We needn't stay long, but I'd like to look in.'

'I haven't got a present,' Sally had objected.

He'd only laughed. 'Just bring yourself, as my guest. It's quite a big affair; that's why she fixed it for a Saturday.'

And here was Sally, ready for the big affair. She'd done her fullest make-up, stroked foundation over her skin, shaped her mouth with lipstick the same colour as her dress, blended pink on her cheeks and green and gold on her eyelids, and finally brushed her lashes with Silk mascara.

And I look all right, she assured herself as she heard the approaching engine. Nothing special, but at least I've made the best of what I've got. I won't disgrace him.

As she'd guessed, the engine was Kemp's. He'd chosen the Range Rover rather than the Mercedes, she noted from her window with surprise, and watched him manoeuvre it skilfully into the tiny flat area which was his only parking space. He jumped out and smiled up at her, raising his arm high from the shoulder in that wide-open greeting which showed how much time he spent outdoors.

'Isn't this great?' He gestured at the reddening sun,

the cloudless sky. 'They couldn't ask for better weather.'

'It's certainly a nice evening,' Sally agreed, glad to share in his contentment.

'Your hair looks pretty.'

'Thanks.' She brushed the clean, scented weight of it from her shoulders. 'I took extra care with the blow-drying.'

'So you're ready?'

'Sure.' She realised he couldn't see the rest of her. 'I'll be right with you.'

Still smiling, Kemp started down the steps. By the time she had tottered downstairs on her spindly heels, he was in at the door.

They met in the wood-panelled hall. This, she realised, was the first time she had seen him in anything but working clothes. That brown tweed jacket still seemed a little casual, but it did go well with the beige shirt and dark brown trousers, and he had combed and flattened his hair.

Sally was about to comment on his lack of a tie when she saw he was frowning. Not the slow, working-things-out frown she had come to recognise, but a scowl which grew ever darker and more thunderous as he took in her appearance.

'What the hell do you think you're wearing?'

She felt her mouth drop open in shock, and closed it tight. How dared he? Yet, even as her own anger flared, even as she squared up to the great, lowering force of his displeasure, her courage failed.

I am *not* frightened of him, she assured herself. Yet she couldn't utter the sharp retort which had risen to her lips, and had to cast round for a less aggressive response.

'Thanks,' she managed at last. 'You certainly know how to encourage a girl!'

'You need encouragement?' Kemp looked her over again from head to foot. 'When you're ready to go out in a postage stamp?'

Sally pulled the wrap over her provocatively displayed breasts, and held it closed in front of her. Aware of how its fringes fell longer than her skirt over her naked tanned legs, she shifted her ankles one behind the other.

'A *gaudy* postage stamp,' he continued relentlessly. 'What would you wear if you really had the courage— a circus outfit?'

'I always wear bright colours.' She hated her defensive tone, but it was the only way she could get it out. 'I'm all sort of muted, myself.'

'I don't know what you mean by muted.' His glance raked her. 'But whatever it is, that stuff on your face doesn't help.'

'I see.' Sally licked her lips, regardless of the carefully applied scarlet. 'So you're an expert on make-up, are you?'

He raised a hand to her painted cheek. 'I know what's real.'

For a moment he stayed there, eyes burning into hers, hand so close she could feel its warmth. Then he snatched it away, and his jaw set in a stubborn line.

'What kind of fool would I be if I didn't?' He turned abruptly from her, and thrust his hands in his pockets. 'After finding out the hard way?'

When he moved again it was at an extravagant saunter, past her and through the open doorway into the living-room. She had an obscure feeling that the argument had veered into some region of his mind where she couldn't follow.

'That's not fair!' she protested.

Released from his presence, she felt much better able to defend herself. Before she knew it, she had kicked off her shoes and hurried after him.

As she'd expected, he was heading for his favourite leather couch. Nimble in her bare feet, she dodged round him and planted herself on the rug in his path. He almost walked into her, and she instinctively put up her hands. They only brushed his jacket, barely enough to feel the roughness of the tweed as she snatched them away, but his recoil was as swift as hers.

'What are you trying to do—make me grab you?' He glared down. 'Would that prove the dress is all right?'

'It would say more about you than about what I'm wearing.' Sally stood her ground, and held on to her sense of his injustice. 'After you've been so rude. . .'

'That wasn't rudeness, it was honesty.'

'All right, so you meant all those ugly things you said.' She swallowed her bitter hurt. 'At least you could have spoken more. . .' She stared up at him, and faltered. 'More nicely,' she finished at last.

How lame it sounded. No wonder the grey-blue eyes had narrowed.

'Some things are more important than party manners.'

'They'd have to be!' she flared. 'Very important indeed, before they mattered more than ordinary human. . .' Once more she hesitated, and at last abandoned the argument for direct attack. 'You were rude,' she rushed on before he could distract her again. 'And the least you can do is be it to my face!'

'Your mask, you mean.' Kemp stared down at it with distaste. 'What are you on about?'

'Th-that stuff about what's real, and finding out the

hard way.' She hesitated, surprised by her own ferocity.
'You were t-talking to somebody else.'

'I'm talking to you. You've ruined yourself.'

'You sound like a Victorian novelette!'

'I'm saying what I damn well mean.'

'You're insulting me, and if that's all you can do I'll
stop caring what you think.' Sally bit her lip, angry
with herself for having admitted she cared at all, and
hurried to cover the blunder. 'My colouring's so
dull——'

'It is now.'

'Oh!' It was one thing to deplore her own looks;
quite another to be so heartily agreed with.

'Dull as a cheap coin.' Kemp pressed home his
advantage. 'One of dozens.'

'A minute ago, you said my hair was. . .' She shook
it back, hating to repeat the word he had used in
kindness.

'I said it was pretty,' he agreed. 'So it was. Is. . .'

He trailed into silence. His glance had followed the
curve of her hair, up from her shoulders to where the
tendrils always played about her ears. She pushed them
back nervously, and the small movement broke the
spell.

'It's just brown now,' he went on with an effort.
'Like anybody's.'

'It always is.' Sally ran her own hand through it,
lifting it from her head to show what she meant.

That proved to be another mistake. He followed the
line of her arm, and then the drift of her hair through
her fingers, and when it was in place he couldn't seem
to tear his glance from her neck and bare shoulders.

When had the shawl dropped from them? And she
couldn't drag it back now. Not now. She resisted the

urge to shield herself from those hot, compelling eyes,
and gabbled any old nonsense that came into her head.

'I once tried red highlights.'

Kemp's eyes widened as awareness came back to
them, and his mouth curled in disgust. 'Yuk!'

'You're a great comfort, you are,' she twittered,
terrified of silence. 'But yes, it was yuk. Not nearly as
bad as the perm and the blonde streaks, though.'

'Don't tell me.' He squinted sideways at her. 'You
must have ended up like Raggedy Ann.'

'Worse. That's when I decided I was stuck with
brown.'

'Beautiful brown,' he corrected.

Oh, dear. Sally concentrated on the tweed of his
jacket, and went on trying. 'You were just saying it
was like anybody's.'

'It wasn't your hair I was getting at, it was this. . .'

He raised a hand to indicate the scanty red silk, and
once more froze in mid-gesture. Slowly, as if against
his will, the palm turned upwards and cupped itself,
until he pulled it back and dropped it to his side.

'Well, I like this red,' she babbled, hardly knowing
what she was saying. 'It's. . .sort of. . .lively.'

It was no use—he was staring at her body again.
Sally huddled herself together, and heard his breath
hiss through his teeth as she tried to shrug her wrap
back into place.

Yes, she'd made it worse. Her breasts were now
gathered and pushed forward, plainly outlined beneath
the flimsy silk. The outlines told more than she wanted
known, and, if that weren't enough, one scarlet strap
was edging its way down her arm. She hurriedly pushed
it up, and dragged the shawl around her any way she
could.

Too late, she remembered its habit of catching in the

clasp of her necklace. Sure enough it did, and stayed
inelegantly twisted at the back of her neck in spite of
all her pulling. With something like panic she felt
Kemp's approach blocking the light.

'Let me.'

His hands stole to her nape, never touching yet
holding her prisoner. Blinded to everything but his
nearness, chin raised over the tweed sleeves, Sally let
his fingertips work at the clasp. It yielded and the beads
parted, a cool amber scratchiness which slid over her
skin and dragged after it the softly brushing wool. He
lifted both away from her, and she drew a trembling
breath.

'It's always doing that.'

His only answer was to drop both, still hopelessly
linked, to the rug. She saw with dismay that his eyes
were half closed, his teeth clenched on the tip of his
tongue.

'Perhaps we'd better. . .' She broke off with a gasp.

His hands were on her at last, pushing at the straps.
She felt a snap, one of them giving way, and the other
retreated down her arm before his stroking, possessing,
irresistible hand.

She never wore a bra; her breasts were too small to
need one. Too small to be proud of, and now so
demanding they shamed her—she couldn't let him see
them like this. She put up a hand, but it came to rest
on his wrist and stayed there, unable to tear itself away
from the smooth line of his shirt-cuff and the warm
play of muscle where it ended.

'You're so strong. . .' It was meant to be a protest,
but it came out a mere whisper.

How could she stop him, when she couldn't even
control her own voice? How could she do anything but
cling to his wrist, not helping, not hindering, while his

hands went on with the work they had set themselves? Slowly, slowly they drew down the silk, past the line of her tan, down again until her breasts raised their twin beacons clear to his view.

She crossed her arms to cover them. 'This isn't me.'

'It is, my darling. It is.'

But he let her go on hiding the two thrusting peaks. He was speeding the dress on its downward journey, pushing, pushing. Something gave with a small ripping sound, and the silk fluttered past her briefs to the floor.

'You're beautiful.'

For an endless moment his eyes devoured her. Then he put an arm under her waist and another under her knees, just as he had that first evening they met. Just as helpless, Sally let him scoop her up, couldn't protest as he lifted her from what had become a mere red tangle round her feet, couldn't speak at all as that wild scent eddied round her and that wide shoulder invited her to rest her head, relax, let it all happen.

Only when he had set her on the couch did her sense of danger return. She stiffened, and braced one hand against the cushions, the other against the bright crochet blanket draped over the back. The blanket's shell pattern crushed against her palm as she summoned her voice in a last effort.

'Please, Kemp!'

But she didn't know what she was pleading for. When his mouth took her breasts she drew herself together, trying to contain the sweetness he set flowing through her.

It would not be contained. She was at his mercy, desolate, hating him, wanting him. His tongue curled and caressed and tormented, and she tangled her fingers in his hair, twisted from side to side, offered each breast anew to this whirlpool of pleasure they had never known till now.

She was sinking, drowning, filled yet emptied, spread and longing to be filled. Kemp's palms tingled on her thighs, teased over her hips, possessed her belly and slid to the waistband of her briefs.

'No!' She sat up, horrified.

His hand stayed where it was, easing gently under the elastic while he tried to take her mouth with his. She struggled away, knowing if he kissed her, if that questing hand reached its goal, she would indeed be defenceless. And she didn't want him, she really didn't, not like this.

'This isn't *me*,' she repeated in desperation. 'You're not loving *me*. I could be just anybody.'

'I won't hurt you,' he murmured in her ear. 'I'll make it wonderful for you—you'll see.'

'And will you marry me if I have a baby?'

'You won't.' Kemp pushed the waistband. 'I'll take care.'

'As you would with anybody. It's not enough.'

'It will be. You'll see.'

'No!' Sally called on all her will with a long, shuddering breath, spread her hands on his chest, and pushed him away.

He only laughed, a low, exulting sound. 'You're afraid because it's the first time. Don't be.'

'Please, Mark, no——'

She broke off in horror, and saw that at last she had made an impression. All the muscles of his face tightened as the passion drained out of him.

'What did you call me?'

The question dropped over her in a quite different voice, heavy and cold. She winced, and drew away from him.

'So he did make a play for you.' He made it a statement, not a question. 'Often?'

'Only. . .only once.'

And why should she feel so guilty about that? She dragged herself from the cushions, swung her feet to the solid cool floor, and spread her hands in a useless attempt to conceal.

'He. . .he never did this to me.'

'And what, exactly,' Kemp spat each word with devastating precision, 'do you mean by *this*?'

Sally quailed. 'I. . . I'm not going to say it.'

He had gone very pale, a pulse beating in his temple. He was furious, and she was naked before his fury, but whose fault was that? She was in the right, she told herself, and tried not to shiver.

'I'm not saying he wouldn't have, but he didn't. And you're. . .you're no better than he is, Kemp Whittaker!'

'What?' He shot to his feet.

She mustn't let him frighten her. If she didn't look at him, if she stood up like this, so she could move quickly if she needed to, then maybe she could say what needed saying.

'You didn't want *me*, you wanted. . .a woman. Any woman.'

She waited for the explosion. When it didn't come she stole a glance and found his mouth pulled in, his eyes unseeing, his anger wrestling and reluctantly giving place to. . .what?

'Damn and blast it, I can't talk while you're like this!' Kemp made one of his decisive moves, and she cowered away. Fearful of tumbling once more to the couch, she shot sideways, dodging round him in the direction of the door, then turned on him with clenched fists.

'Don't touch me,' she quavered. 'I'll fight. . .'

'No need for that.'

She saw he had lifted the blanket from the back of the couch. He flicked it open, held it before him like a matador's cape, and advanced on her. As he neared her, he raised it higher and turned away as if he couldn't bear to look at her, but still imperiously shook the blanket.

'Turn round.'

Sally obeyed without a second thought and the blessed folds dropped round her. She settled them at her neck, bunched them in front not to trip over them, and felt her whole body relax as she faced him again.

'Now.' He gestured with absurd formality to the great armchair. 'Would you care for a seat?'

She drew herself up, haughty as a duchess. 'I don't think we've anything more to say to each other.'

'Like hell we haven't!' He dropped on the couch, well away from her. 'You've just roused me like a——'

'Don't you dare call me names!' she interrupted in a fury. 'It wasn't *my* idea to start all that!'

'It was you who wore this.'

Kemp gestured with his foot at the crumpled dress. Righteously indignant in her sheltering blanket, she stared scornfully back at him.

'I should be able to wear what I like!'

'Not that one, Sally, please.'

'Well, shouldn't I?'

'This thing's like a sign at the door.' His foot pushed the scrap of silk towards her. 'Can you wonder I wanted to come in and enjoy myself?'

'Oh! How. . .how dare you?' Eyes wide with shock and disgust, Sally remembered her argument and grabbed it. 'And doesn't that show exactly what I

mean? All you wanted was. . .was sex. Anybody would
have done!'

Had she made an impression? Yes, he was staring at
her now with the beginning of that familiar, considering
frown. Even if he wouldn't admit her argument, he saw
it, she was sure.

'As a matter of fact,' he began slowly, 'I'm pretty
choosy.'

'You know perfectly well what I mean.' She ventured
a toe out of her blanket to edge the dress aside. 'You
weren't with *me*. I don't know who was on your
mind. . .'

'Jacqui used to be fond of clothes like that.' Kemp
leant back on the leather cushions, and stared out to
the sunset-coloured mountains. 'Different styles, but
always. . .tantalising.'

'I did wonder.' Sally heard her own voice drop in
depression. 'So it's her I was standing in for!'

'I didn't say that.'

'Did she manage to make you take no for an
answer?'

He laughed without mirth, a small explosion of
bitterness. 'If you only knew!'

'So you listened when *she* talked about. . .' unable
to face him, determined to get it out, Sally fixed her
attention on the blue-pink sky outside the other
window '. . .about babies?'

'She never mentioned them. Most women don't.'

Sally nodded. Jacqui Lane, and the other women
he'd been involved with, must have seen to their own
protection. With this hot-blooded, headlong, power-
fully attractive partner, it would only be common
sense.

Why, she wondered as she had so many times before,
could she never bring herself to take the same steps?

Was it because, deep down, she knew she could never settle for anything less than the most a man could offer?

'You did ask her to marry you,' she reminded him, cautious of the violent reaction she had provoked last time she spoke of this.

'Didn't I just!'

He sprang upright, paced to the padded corner-bench round the table, and flung himself on it. Sally waited, newly alarmed by the strength of feeling revealed in the explosive words, the clenched muscles, the eyes staring across the valley to the purple-pink mountains. When he spoke again, it was very softly.

'She set me up, you know. That intercom was all part of it.'

Sally saw that this was something he wanted to talk about. And if he wanted it, she realised with surprise, so did she.

'Why,' she asked gently, 'would anyone do a thing like that?'

'To get known. The firm's drama group had given her a taste for acting, and she meant to go professional.'

'She already was known—as your girlfriend.'

'Girlfriends are small stuff. She was after headlines—planned them the minute we met.' Kemp kept his head turned away from her, his eyes fixed on the distant mountains. 'After that business with the intercom, the offers rolled in. She didn't need me any more.'

Hearing the bitterness in the bleak, jerky sentences, Sally kept her voice low. 'But wasn't it you who finished it?'

He shook his head, still staring out of the window. 'But there wasn't much I could do to contradict her, once she'd given her story to the Press.'

Sally traced a pattern on the carpet with her bare toe. 'Are you still in love with her?'

Why should the idea make her feel so hollow and deprived? And why should her blood surge as she watched that vigorous shake of the head that set his wild hair flying?

'I never was with her, only with the idea of her, what she made me believe.' He sighed. 'That was hard to shake off.'

'But you have?'

The deep-set eyes kindled. 'You, of all people, shouldn't need to ask that.'

'I do, though. You wanted to marry her.' Returned squarely to her own problems, Sally faced him across the room. 'You haven't said anything about marriage to me.'

He frowned in surprise. 'You surely don't expect me to, after five days?'

'Yet you expected me to. . .' She looked down, aware of her burning cheeks. 'I wouldn't want that after five days either.'

'I know.' He fully accepted the point she was making—she could tell by his subdued tone. 'And I'd have had more sense, only that dress. . .' He trailed off. 'I'm not going to make excuses. But face it, Sally, you were giving the wrong signals.'

And because he had admitted his own fault, she could see where she herself had gone wrong. She remembered with a new shame why she had chosen the dress. How out of place it had felt in the hotel restaurant when she'd worn it for dinner after the day's work. Yes, and how she'd had to flee from Harry in the bar afterwards, and had changed with relief into her tracksuit for that fateful evening jog.

'Maybe it is all wrong for me.' She stooped to the

fragile scrap of silk and found, as she had feared, a jagged rip at the waist. 'Whether it is or not, I won't be able to wear it now.'

'It wouldn't do for tonight anyway,' Kemp told her. 'I explained the minute I saw it——'

'Explained?' She gave him an ironic glance, though it was rather spoilt when her blanket fell apart and she had to grab its edges. Nevertheless, she followed it up. 'That was explaining?'

'I do express myself a bit strongly sometimes.' Kemp met her eyes ruefully. 'I didn't mean to upset you.'

'A circus outfit. A mask.' She bent once more, to gather up her necklace and shawl. 'Dull as a cheap coin, one of dozens——'

'But can't you see?' he broke in heatedly. 'You aren't one of dozens, that's why it matters. You were covering up the real, only you——'

'Cue for song!' Now that all her finery was back in her charge, she found it easier to be flippant.

His smile was reluctant at first, then lifted and lightened all the lines of his eyes. 'Was I winding myself up again?'

'You were, though this time it was nice.' She looked down, making a great business of readjusting the blanket. 'Only we do have to get on, so what do I wear? This is. . .*was*,' she amended, 'the only dress I have with me.'

'So put on your jeans, and whatever's your usual make-up.'

'For a party?'

'I suppose I should have explained,' he admitted. 'But believe me, the more casual you are for it, the better.'

At least it was easy, and quick. When she came down for the second time, he nodded approval at her silk shirt, a rich coral pink but severely plain, and passed her deep blue trainers and her belt with the silver buckle as exactly right.

'You're you again,' he commented, opening the passenger door of the Range Rover. 'Welcome back.'

'It's certainly more comfortable.' Sally settled beside him, then blinked as he manoeuvred into the road. 'We're going *uphill*? But there's only forest.'

'Forest, pastures, farms. Dr Elise lives on one of those, half a mile away.'

'She bought it?'

'Bought nothing. Her husband inherited it, and works it.'

'But with everything so steep, isn't that fearfully hard?'

'The Swiss are a mountain people.' Kemp guided the vehicle along the narrow road between lush, unfenced meadows that tipped at dramatic angles. 'They take hard work for granted.'

They'd have to, Sally decided when she saw the land round the farm. It all went steeply up or steeply down. Not one of this crowd under the fir trees could cross a space to greet a friend without climbing or descending. As for those children kicking a football wouldn't they be always having to run downhill for it?

The tiny level strip in front of the house already held a coach and two minibuses. Kemp parked with practised ease at what seemed like an impossible angle by a wood-pile.

'We should have walked—most people did from the village.' He jumped out and came round to pull open her door against the force of gravity. 'Only we—er—left it a bit late.'

'Still,' she clambered out, grateful he was having to

give all his attention to holding open the tipped-up door, 'I'm glad you—er—made me change.'

The Camuzzi farm was of the same old silvery wood as Kemp's, but bigger and at the moment much noisier. A tiny girl staggered up to the road and embraced Sally's knees, closely followed by another of perhaps eleven, who murmured what sounded like an apology and carried the squirming toddler down the steps and round the corner of the house. Where they had vanished, two small boys with waving guns sprang out as though by a conjuring trick, and were called off with authority by a lean, grey-haired man.

'Your host,' Kemp told Sally.

She shook the proffered hand, and smiled while Kemp exchanged a few quick words with Dr Elise's husband.

'He says we're to make ourselves at home,' he told her.

Sally nodded her thanks, and they entered the front door into a purposeful whirlwind. The living-room seemed quieter, but Kemp drew Sally away from it.

'The old folk are in there, reminiscing with cronies they only see at times like this.'

He guided her instead to a huge kitchen, smelling deliciously of coffee and hot bread and fruit, and milling with capable-looking women. One or two had overalls over neat dresses, many were clad in trousers and shirts like Sally's, others wore blouses and bright skirts. Dr Elise emerged from their midst, looking almost formal in pleated blue linen.

'I'm so glad your knee is better, my dear.' She shook Sally's hand. 'Welcome to my half-century.'

'I'm honoured to be asked,' murmured Sally, and meant it.

'Kemp!' Dr Elise pushed up her silver spectacles for

a stern glance. 'Later, we speak of that check-up you do not come for.'

'I take my own blood-pressure regularly,' Kemp assured her. 'It's been copybook normal for months.'

'So our mountain life suits you.' The doctor nodded in satisfaction, and became a hostess again. 'Is good. You may take Miss Benedict to the cellar.'

'The cellar?' Sally repeated in an undertone as Kemp led her along a corridor.

'Only part of it, the rest's still farm storage space.'

He drew her aside, and they pressed to the wall to allow a smiling woman to pass them. Her board held assorted cheeses interspersed with white grapes and black, prunes, parsley, slices of green and red peppers. She was followed by another with a great wheel of brown bread, and a third with dishes of butter.

'And what was that about blood-pressure?' Sally asked.

'I suppose the life I used to lead didn't suit me. You may have noticed.' Kemp gave her a rueful grin. 'I kind of fly off the handle quite easily.'

'You are just a wee bit combustible,' she agreed, and paused at the top of a stone flight of steps. 'Are you here for your health, then?'

'Only indirectly. Here, I'll go first down these. I visited two years ago,' he called back over his shoulder as he descended. 'To make that programme about marmots—do you remember it? Then I gradually dug in.'

'So you don't live in London any more?'

'I keep a flat there, for when I need it. Which seems to be less and less.'

The sound of voices swelled, and he opened the door for her into the wide, apple-scented space which was clearly the focus of the party. The room was a cellar only in the most technical sense. On this steep land, the lower storey had been built into the slope. It probably got as much light as anywhere in the house, though with the swiftly darkening sky outside, it was hard to tell at the moment. As Kemp and Sally passed the white-draped, loaded table, soft lights blinked on round the walls.

Without needing to ask each other, they continued to where the double doors stood open to the grassy space outside. This too was lit now, with strings of lanterns. Up on the road, more guests were arriving in the village taxi. Its headlights glared intrusively, and Sally was glad to turn away from them and rest her eyes again on the soft-lit groups scattered under the trees.

At the foot of one, middle-aged men gossiped comfortably on a bench. Near another, a teenage boy plucked a guitar, a girl sang softly, and the same toddler who had so lovingly saluted Sally's knees now bobbed enchantingly to their music. A little away from them, another child slept in the arms of a man who was presumably her father, and laughter rose from a group of young people round a table which had somehow been made to stand upright. It was an extraordinary scene in its way, Sally thought: festive yet quiet, full of the tranquil enjoyment of a people who knew the value of peace and had guarded it for centuries.

Which made it all the more of a shock when her attention was drawn again to the new arrivals. The taxi's tail-lights sped away down the hill, leaving two dream-like figures, pale yet absurdly smooth and glossy in this rustic setting, to pick their way over the grass towards her.

'Mark!' Sally gasped. 'Tara! What are you doing here?'

CHAPTER FIVE

'Kemp, old lad, how are you?'

Mark raised an arm in confident greeting. The jacket of his light suit parted over a dark shirt and flame-coloured tie, designed to be eye-catching even at this distance in this light.

'Hi, Sally,' he added as an afterthought.

Sally glanced at Kemp, and saw the swift anger gathering between his brows. Then the frown vanished as quickly as it had come, and he sent a frosty nod up the slope.

'What on earth are you doing here?' she called out nervously. 'I didn't know you knew Dr Elise.'

'Dr Camuzzi, you mean?' Mark seemed to be wondering whether to come straight down to them. 'She takes care of the hotel guests.' He tested the thick turf with a well-polished shoe. 'That'll soon include my clients.'

'You mean she's asked you here to talk business?'

'Elise wouldn't do that,' Kemp growled into her ear.

Sally flushed, conscious that her voice and Mark's had been too loud in this peaceful gathering. To her relief, Elise's husband was ascending the steps to greet the newcomers.

'She would ask them out of ordinary hospitality. But our friend over there wouldn't understand anything like——' Kemp broke off, then spoke again with measured calm. 'Who's the woman?'

'My assistant.' Sally felt her spirits dropping to zero.

'She doesn't seem old enough.' He took in Tara's charming fragility. 'Or tough enough.'

'Thank you. So to do my job, you have to be old and tough?'

He glanced at her in surprise. 'What's the matter with you? Can't I comment on your pretty friend——'

'Colleague,' she corrected him frostily.

'You don't like her.' He made it a statement rather than a question, and shrugged. 'I suppose there has to be something wrong with her, to stand a whole weekend with that phoney.'

'That ph——' Sally stopped, exasperated to find herself about to use his word. 'Mark Walsh happens to be Tara's client. And mine.'

'Isn't this where we came in?' Kemp's gaze strayed once more to Tara. 'And she *is* pretty.'

Chilled, Sally watched the newcomers follow their host down to the house. Tara did seem superbly young, slender and sparkling as a mischievous schoolgirl with her flyaway blonde curls and pleated black tunic. Tapping down the steps in her high heels, she attracted indulgent, amused glances from men and women alike. Mark lounged after her with his usual lean elegance, but only the women returned his brilliant, all-purpose smiles.

'I wonder what he's after?' Kemp speculated.

Sally bit her lip. Could he really not guess? She stared up at him, but he had stepped aside to make way for the small groups who were starting to drift to the supper-table. He now had his back to the brightly-lit party room, and the deep-set, shadowy eyes gave no clue to what he was thinking.

'Kingfisher d-does have business here.' Hearing her own nervous stammer, she took a grip on herself. 'I suppose he's tying up loose ends. Like the one about medical care——'

'Medical care,' Kemp interrupted with a return of the familiar impatience, 'is easily fixed in office hours.'

'There could be other things,' she almost pleaded. 'He might just fancy a weekend in a beautiful place.'

'Not this kind of beautiful place.'

A passing guest paused to shake hands. Sally saw with surprise that it was the hotel manager, looking quite different in open-necked shirt and light trousers. She returned his greeting politely, and assured him that she was much better. He moved on and she glanced at Kemp, hoping the interruption had made him forget what they had been talking about.

No such luck. He turned towards her, his craggy face edged here and there with brightness.

'You've worked with Mark Walsh. Do you really think he'd like a place as quiet as Engeldorf?'

Defeated, Sally lowered her gaze. Why was she arguing anyway? Any minute now Mark and Tara would be with them, and then she'd have to face her problem full on.

'And if he did,' Kemp pointed out with ruthless logic, 'he's the last person to spend his time here socialising with a country doctor and a small farmer.'

She sought for a retort, and found none.

'On the other hand,' Kemp continued, 'he seems pretty keen to make out that he's a buddy of mine.'

She jerked her head up in startled dismay. 'That's just his way. He does it with everybody.'

'Everybody?' The deep voice rose in ironic question. 'He hardly bothered to give you the time of day.'

'He. . .he may be a bit annoyed with me.'

She noted with relief that Kemp wasn't going to ask why. He had his own ideas to pursue.

'And he was damned condescending to Georg Camuzzi. But then,' the reasoning drew to a bleak conclusion, 'Georg isn't so useful in the sacred cause of promoting Mark Walsh.'

'I really don't think he's that bad.'

'He's here for publicity, isn't he?'

She sighed, giving up. 'That's about it.'

'Have you any idea why he's brought along your sidekick?'

She had, but didn't want to speak of it. If Tara had already taken over the Kingfisher account, she would be ready to absorb Sally's other accounts, and her desk, and her job. It was too much to think about all at once.

Perhaps some of her misery showed in her face. Kemp didn't let the subject go, but his voice grew unexpectedly gentle.

'Would you care to tell me what you do know?'

'He wants. . .' Sally broke off, swallowed, forced it out. 'He wants your name on the brochures.' She waited for the explosion. When it didn't come, she hurried on, 'Your *Truth* programme's very hot on conservation. And the Kingfisher holidays here. . .'

'Are carefully controlled,' he finished for her, still with that new gentleness. 'The Swiss would see to that.'

She peered up at him, wishing she could make out more of his features. 'You don't sound angry.'

'It's a waste of. . .' Kemp paused, and shrugged '. . .of everything, being angry with the Mark Walshes of this world.'

Of everything? Why didn't he say of time, or of energy, if that was what he meant? With a sudden chill, she remembered Dr Elise's strictures about his blood-pressure. Perhaps he'd had to learn to go easy on himself, not to care too much about things he couldn't change. Was that why he hadn't blown up when Mark had arrived? Was it a technique he used, to relax out of trouble by turning his mind to other subjects?

To pretty girls like Tara, for instance?

She'd be much better for him than me, Sally realised with a pang. She never argues.

No, Tara would never shout and quarrel. She got her way by coaxing, and flattering, and pleasing. Whatever the problem, she would always plan a way round it, find a strategy, and come out ahead.

She'd never get into the mess I'm in now, Sally thought, raging at her own incompetence. For a start, she wouldn't stray too far and too late in the forest. . .

But that brought a new idea, and new pain. If Kemp wasn't supposed to get excited, how much damage had her own intrusion done him that night? And all the times since, when she'd noisily fallen out with him, and this evening when she'd stopped him. . .

But I had to, she told herself desperately. It was all wrong. Think about something else.

Which wasn't easy. She was almost glad when Kemp resumed his dogged probing.

'So Walsh wants my co-operation, but didn't trust you to get it?' He waited for her miserable agreement before he went on. 'We know why he's here, then.'

Sally nodded, more despondent than ever. 'He must have decided to come here right after we talked yesterday.'

'With a little help from your. . .' he left an ironic pause '. . .from your colleague.'

'Tara suits him better than I do,' she admitted with difficult honesty.

'Maybe that's——'

'Kemp, you old hermit!' Mark's sharp voice cut through their sombre mood, as his bright clothes and

hair cut through the soft light. 'No wonder you're so
hard to find nowadays! What's it like, living at the top
of a mountain?'

'I wouldn't know.' Kemp's answer was quiet, controlled. 'You'd better go a thousand metres higher, and
ask the chamois.'

Mark's practised party-laugh rang out, and he turned
to draw Tara into their group. 'Come on, love, now's
your chance. She's dying to meet you,' he added to
Kemp. 'She's been a fan of yours ever since you
started, when she was twelve.'

Which would make her about twenty now, Sally
thought cynically. But why not? Tonight she looks even
younger.

Aloud, she did her best to greet her assistant with
decent politeness. 'Is this work or pleasure?'

'This part—pure pleasure.' Tara turned at once to
Kemp. 'What a thrill!'

'She's helping on the campaign,' Mark gave Sally a
meaningful glance, 'seeing that we couldn't reach you.'

'You're so *big*!' Tara breathed, fluffy head tilted
back, blue eyes widening at Kemp's great height.
'*Much* bigger than you look on screen.'

'It's all relative.'

Kemp's face was still in shadow, but Sally noted with
a pang how his voice had relented. However much he
might suspect this innocent eagerness, he couldn't help
responding to it. Any man would.

'In the studio I mostly sit down,' he went on. 'And
in the wild. . .'

'I know,' Tara nodded wisely. 'There aren't any
other humans to compare with you.'

'Exactly. Only things like trees, and badgers.'

'And wolves!' Tara's pink lips parted in renewed

excitement. 'You were so *brave*! You went so *close* to them.'

She'd certainly done her homework, Sally decided with reluctant admiration. How many videos had Tara got hold of and watched in a hurry?

'I'm never as near the animals as it looks,' Kemp was assuring her. 'The telescopic lens——'

'Tara knows about those,' Sally put in briskly.

All eyes turned to her, and she realised she had sounded like a disapproving nanny. She tried for a lighter tone.

'We work with photographers. It's part of the job.'

'Hey,' Mark rushed in as if to cover a gaffe, 'how about us all having lunch tomorrow? Can the hotel up here put on a really great meal?'

'I'd be surprised if it can't,' Sally began.

'Of course it can,' Kemp said at the same time.

She peered up at his dark outline. Was he feeling as irritated as herself? Had he picked up the patronising hint that out here in the sticks, you mustn't expect too much? She couldn't tell.

'Right,' Mark pressed on. 'Then we'll have the best the old place can produce, yes?'

Kemp's enigmatic, shadowed eyes turned towards Sally. She licked her lips, unable to speak.

'A kind of thank-you,' Mark nodded sideways at her, 'for all you've done to help our Sal here.'

Sally winced. Would she ever find the courage to say how she hated being called Sal? She gazed up at Kemp, pleading with him not to hold all this against her. She still couldn't see his eyes, yet somehow she knew they were on her, reading her.

'OK,' he growled at last. 'I mean—er—thanks, I'll come.'

'Ooh, how exciting!' Tara clasped her hands grace-fully before her modestly displayed bosom. 'I've not only *met* Kemp Whittaker, I'm having *lunch* with him!'

Mark had raised both fists to shoulder-height in an instinctive gesture of triumph. As Sally watched he thought better of it, and started instead to loosen his tie. 'Dr Camuzzi didn't tell me how informal we were going to be.' He tucked the tie in his top pocket, then took off his jacket and slung it over his shoulder. 'That's more like it.'

Sally let her eyes linger on the well-muscled torso. The tailored shirt fitted neatly, its colour subtle as a dark flame and setting off to perfection his smooth tan. Much too smooth, she decided, reminded of her early suspicion that he used a sunbed.

I haven't thought about that since the first time I ever saw him, she marvelled to herself. I expect he works out regularly in the gym too. He isn't out scrambling about in all weathers, like. . .

She turned to Kemp, startled by his quick move-ment. As if to prove how fit you could keep by just scrambling about in all weathers, he had dropped to reach for something on the turf.

Tara must have stepped out of her shoes. He rose in the same easy movement, displaying one of the tiny, exotic, absurdly feminine objects in each great hand.

'How do you women get about on these things?' he wanted to know.

'It isn't easy.' Tara fluttered her lashes. 'But there's generally somebody to hold on to.'

Three inches shorter, she looked sweeter and more delicate than ever. She somehow managed to make five feet two the only height to be as she turned and tiptoed out over the turf like a little girl exploring.

'Come on!' she called back to Kemp. 'I'm longing to try that seat under the trees!'

From the way she said it, they must have already settled that they were going to. Kemp took a step after her, and spoke in a low voice. Sally was still trying to make out the words when a firm grip on her arm drew her away, into the party room.

'Leave them be, sweetie,' murmured Mark, his breath warm and spicy in her ear. 'Let's go and eat.'

'I. . . I'm not hungry.'

Unable to free her arm, she craned round. Sure enough, Kemp had turned to stare at them, his face at last brightly lit and that frown once more between his brows. The long mouth tightened in—could it be disgust?

'A drink, then,' Mark persisted.

'I'm not thirsty.'

'Thirsty nothing! You need to loosen up, Sal.'

Kemp turned abruptly and strode out across the turf. The shoes, clamped together by their heels, fluttered from his hand like small birds. Struggling between rage and a bitter sense of loss, Sally watched him fling himself down beside Tara on the furthest of the wooden benches. The fluffy bright head shone in the dimness, and presently the shaggy dark one bent close to it.

Sally turned her back on them, but the view in this direction was no better. Mark was staring complacently past her.

'Now there's real talent.' He sounded respectful, almost reverent. 'You ought to study her methods, Sal, while you've got the chance.'

'Then you've given her the account?' she asked, failure harsh in her mouth.

'You keep jumping the gun,' he scolded in high good

humour. 'She might get the agreement we want, she might not. He's an oddball, that Whittaker.'

'Because he cares about exploited creatures?' she flared. 'Because he won't live in cities, and spend his time——?'

'Steady on!' Mark raised an arm in mock defence. 'I was only trying to tell you why we still need you.'

'You do?'

Sally found she was breathing a little fast. She had been ready to burn her boats. Resigned to losing the account, she had been about to launch a defence of Kemp, which would at the same time have been an attack on Mark and on the whole smug way of life which allowed him to call Kemp an 'oddball'.

Now she found that way of life might still be hers, if she could hang on to it. Did she want to?

Of course I do, she told herself drearily. It's a living, isn't it? What else am I fit for?

'You've been around Whittaker for days,' Mark was explaining. 'You must have learnt a thing or two about him that we can use.'

Repelled by the idea, Sally gritted her teeth. 'Maybe.'

'So you're still in a stronger position than Tara,' Mark pointed out. 'For the moment, anyway.'

For the moment. She knew exactly what that meant. An hour ago she had angrily accused Kemp of wanting her just because she was a woman. Now another woman had turned up, attractive and eager to please and probably—she flinched from the thought, but it had to be faced—probably more than willing to go to bed with him. It wasn't hard to guess what would happen next.

'Besides, who knows what'll happen next?' Mark unconsciously echoed her dismal thoughts. 'Tara's a great little operator, and she's not putting it on. She really does fancy Whittaker a lot.'

'She does? Well,' Sally heard herself gabbling, 'I s-suppose he must have plenty of f-fans.'

Anything to cover the thumping of her heart. Its message pounded through her veins with a new, hopeless longing. Of course Tara fancied Kemp—any woman would. He wasn't just attractive in the ordinary way; he was unique. Who else was so downright, so honest, so very much the man of truth in every sense?

'And she'll certainly turn in her job if she marries him,' Mark went on.

'If she *what*?' Sally licked her lips, trying to recover her composure. 'Aren't *you* jumping the gun a bit?'

'You know our Tara. What she wants, she gets.'

'And. . .that's what she wants?'

He nodded. 'We've talked.'

'But she's only just met him!'

'You really should take lessons, Sal. The first meeting's when you make your impact.'

'But marriage. . . How does she know it would work?'

'Of course it'll work!' Mark exclaimed, contemptuously surprised at her ignorance. 'He's rich and famous, isn't he? Just what the doctor ordered.'

'For a whole lifetime?'

'Who said anything about a lifetime?' The green eyes shone with cynical amusement. 'Honestly, Sal. . .though, come to think of it,' he added on a more calculating note, 'you could be right. She certainly feels that way at the moment.'

'I'm. . . I'm glad to hear it,' muttered Sally, and tried to be. Hadn't she herself just concluded that Tara might be very good for Kemp?

'But lifetimes don't come into it—a year or two's all

she needs.' Mark dismissed the subject for one which interested him more. 'I suppose you've nothing going with Whittaker yourself?'

Numbed, she shook her head.

'I thought not. You'd have spiked Tara, if you'd already got your hooks in him.'

Sally felt the swift colour flooding into her cheeks. She drew herself up, provoked at last into saying what she thought.

'That's a hideous way of putting it!'

'Sorry, love,' he apologised equably. 'You're looking good, do you know that? Mountain air suits you.'

She longed to crane round, to see what was going on under the distant trees. Instead, she had to stare into those glittering green eyes which had once held her spellbound.

'So,' she floundered back to the only thing about him that interested her any more, 'I still have the account?'

'If you can handle it this time.'

His fingers stole to her inner elbow, sliding lightly over the tender flesh under her coral-pink sleeve. She looked down and thought back to the time when this hand, caressing her like this, would have set her senses whirling.

'What a fool I was.' She was surprised, and startled, to find she had spoken the words aloud.

'Mm,' he agreed complacently. 'So Whittaker's taught you that much, has he?'

'You could say so.'

She moved her arm, overcome by a wave of distaste. Why was she hanging about here, where everything had gone sour? She would leave the party, get away from Mark, find her way back to the stars and the earth scents and the huge calm of the mountains.

'I've. . .' she grasped at an excuse '. . . I've got to pack. Kemp said we'd only spend a short time here.'

Mark glanced past her. 'I don't think *he'll* want to leave yet.'

Sally stared up at the satisfied green eyes with a dull dislike. 'Perhaps I'll just find Dr Elise, and make my excuses.'

'Good idea,' he agreed, prompt as if he had expected it. 'Shall I phone the taxi?'

She managed a short laugh, low and throaty but reasonably convincing. 'It's only ten minutes' walk!'

'In the dark?'

'The moon's up.'

Sally stepped out into the night, and managed not to look at the seat under the far trees. Instead, she threw back her head, soothed already by the almost-full moon which hung above the white peaks on the other side of the valley.

'It'll be beautiful on the road,' she added. 'The meadows are full of flowers.'

The flowers would be cut for hay in a few days. Kemp had told her how the fragrance of it would be everywhere as you walked round the village. By then, though, she reminded herself dismally, she'd be back among the traffic fumes.

Dr Elise was hard to find. At last Sally located her in an upper room, cradling a tired child and chatting to a much younger woman who was shaking out a tiny pair of pyjamas. She accepted Sally's farewell with absent-minded good nature, and wished her a pleasant journey home. Sally left the house with her eyes resolutely ahead, not looking for Kemp, taking the steps two at a time in her relief to be alone again.

Only she wasn't alone. City shoes pattered after her,

and Mark drew indignantly to her side, shrugging into his jacket.

'Why didn't you wait?' he demanded. 'I was sweet-talking the old boy.'

'You mean Mr Camuzzi?' She stepped out in a fury.

'It doesn't hurt to stay on good terms.' He easily kept pace with her. 'They own some of the forest, did you know?'

'Most people in the village do,' she told him, surprised to find how much she had learnt during her stay. 'A bit here, a bit there. They look after it for the timber.'

But he wasn't interested in village economy. He wanted to talk of the new package he was putting together: shark fishing in the Gulf of Mexico. Reflecting that he should have named his firm Sharkfisher, or even just Shark, Sally fumed along at top speed. With him at her side, she could find no peace in the keen air, the moon-white mountains, the twinkling lights of the valley. She might as well get home as quickly as possible.

Home! She halted at Kemp's farmhouse in a new wave of misery. If only it were! If only Kemp had given her this key to keep, instead of just to use during her short—too short—stay.

'Well,' in spite of her dismal thoughts, she drew it from her pocket with relief, 'this is where——'

'Where it gets interesting.' Mark lifted the key from her astonished fingers, went down the steps, and opened the door with a flourish. 'Come on! What are you waiting for?'

'You can't go in there!' she gasped. 'It's——'

'It's ours, I gather. Isn't he sleeping up at the castle?'

'But. . .but. . .'

'And tonight,' Mark added with an impatient jerk of

his head at the open doorway, 'he certainly won't be alone up there.'

Helpless, Sally let her leaden feet drag her down the steps. By the time she had reached the door he was already inside, switching on lights. She had no choice but to follow him into the living-room.

'Nice.' He looked round at the quietly luxurious furniture. 'Might that be the bar?'

'N-no,' she told him, though she'd never looked inside the carved pinewood cupboard. 'I. . . I don't know that there are any drinks here at all.'

It was true, she realised with surprise. In all the time she'd been here, she and Kemp had never drunk anything stronger than lemonade together.

'You'd think alcohol was illegal or something!' He adjusted the switches, the side-lamps glowing through their plaited shades as the ceiling light went out. 'There wasn't a thing to be had at that party but coffee and fruit juice.'

'I didn't notice.'

'Not interested, eh?' Mark dropped his hand from the switch, and advanced on her. 'Well, there are other ways.'

'Ways of what?' She retreated before him until she had to stop, her way barred by the table.

'Of enjoying yourself, of course.'

He seized her waist. She tried to recoil, but the solid edge of the table cut into the backs of her thighs, and his hands bit into her flesh, merciless as the grapples of a machine.

He strained against her, shutting out the rest of the room. 'See what you do to me, love?'

'Don't use that word!' she hissed, choking on his wretched, spicy aftershave. 'You don't begin to. . .mmm. . .mmm. . .'

His mouth had fastened on hers. Had there really been a time when she had welcomed these kisses? The very idea shamed her. In lovemaking, as in everything else, Mark was single-minded, self-centred, seeking nothing but his own pleasure. Undeterred by her resistance, perhaps even unaware of it, he pried at her lips with his tongue. She tried to pull away, failed, tried again to protest, and realised too late that she should never have opened her mouth. All she could manage was a muffled squeak as his tongue, tasting of cigars and peppermint and antiseptic, claimed hers.

Trust him to use a mouthwash! she thought savagely. Getting his flavour out of a bottle, instead of bringing it with him from the forest, like. . .

But she couldn't name that name, even to herself. Not here, not now, not like this.

At last Mark released her mouth, though he kept tight hold of her. Closed in the unwanted circle of his grip, she fought for air and turned her head away from him.

'Come on, Sal,' he scolded. 'You want the account, don't you? You *said* you could handle it this time.'

She froze. 'I. . . I didn't realise. . .'

'I thought that would make you see sense. Now relax, or you're no good to a man.'

'You've got it all wrong. I don't reckon to be. . .' she hesitated on the self-centred phrase '. . .to be good to a man.'

'No?' He sounded surprised. 'Didn't you say Whittaker had taught you a thing or two?'

'Not this kind of thing or two!'

'And he's had you about the place this long?' The surprise turned to disbelief. 'Is there something wrong with him?'

'The opposite.' Sally gazed over his shoulder at the

room which until now had always been so welcoming. 'He's. . .'

She broke off. How could she explain the qualities which made Kemp such a special human being? How could Mark, with his limited vision and his self-serving vanity, understand the value of someone who tried to see the other person's point of view, who cared and conserved and protected instead of snatching at whatever he wanted? Why, even to have allowed this hustler into Kemp's home, however unwillingly, seemed a kind of betrayal.

I must get him out, she thought, and did her best to sound calm and decisive. 'You'd better go now,' she said aloud.

'Wait!' Mark lowered his eyelids, smug in the tiny world which was all he knew. 'I think I'm starting to see it. You've never had a man, have you?'

Sally raised her chin and stared full into the hard eyes so near, so intrusively near her own. 'I don't see why I should——'

'That's why Whittaker left you alone, isn't it?'

'Will you please let me go?'

'Virgins aren't everybody's cup of tea,' he went on as if she hadn't spoken. 'I wouldn't have bothered either, if I'd known. Still, here I am.' He plucked at her shirt, and ground his body into hers. 'All set to do you a favour.'

She caught uselessly at his wrists, trying to overcome a new, ugly fear. 'Stop that! I don't want——'

'Oh, yes, you do.' He flicked expertly at her buttons. 'Be sensible, now. This won't be much fun for me, remember.'

Should she scream? No, it wouldn't help, even if she could be heard through these thick old timbers. The next house was well down the hillside, and who would be passing on the quiet road? Not Kemp, who by this time was probably safe in the castle with Tara. At the thought of those two together in that giant's lair, that private kingdom where she had never been invited, Sally's heart twisted.

After all, she thought in despair, why not let this happen? It has to, some time. And at least it'll help me keep the account.

'That's better.' Sensing her compliance, Mark drew back her shirt from her small breasts. 'Now we can go places, sweetie.'

'Only if you've. . .' She stammered to silence, and tried again. 'I don't. . . I'm not. . .protected. . .'

She couldn't go on. She hated the sound of her own voice, hated the words which brought the act one step closer and made it real, hated Mark's smug smile as he tapped his upper pocket.

'Ever ready, that's me.' He raised an enquiring eyebrow. 'Your room?'

'I. . . I suppose so.' She let him draw her out to the hall, but paused at the foot of the stairs. 'I'm still not sure. . .'

'Now, now, none of that! Tell you what, maybe this'll help.'

He set his mouth to one of her breasts, and she stood quiet, trying to enjoy it. It wasn't like Kemp, but maybe that didn't matter. Maybe it would be all right. . .

She stiffened. 'You're hurting!'

'Only a little.' Mark straightened up, laughing. 'You'll get used to it. In fact,' he shrugged out of his jacket with lazy confidence, and draped it over the stair-rail, 'in no time at all, you'll be liking it.'

Eyes holding hers, he kicked off his shoes. Sally stared back at him, one hand on her smarting breast.

Stoats do this, she thought confusedly. They do it to rabbits, so they can eat them.

Was she really going to hold still and be eaten? She must be mad even to think of it. Mad to have got this far at all with this cheap show-off, this tinpot Casanova, this stoat-man who understood nothing but how to eat rabbits. A wave of revulsion washed over her, so strong it left her physically sick.

'I. . . I need some air,' she said faintly.

Hardly aware of what she was doing, she stumbled to the door and opened it wide on the rising, moonlit garden. He joined her, and the confused outline of a plan formed, as much in her senses as in her outraged mind.

'The moon isn't quite full yet,' she babbled, spilling out any words that came into her head. 'It won't be, until tomorrow or the next day——'

'Come on, sweetie!' Mark moved to close the door, pushing her out of the way with an arm in front of her. 'We've got things to get on with.'

Sally stepped back in apparent obedience, waiting her moment.

This was it! Hardly knowing what she was doing, impelled by fear, hatred, and the sense of danger, she set both hands between his shoulder-blades and pushed for all she was worth.

And it worked. Taken by surprise, he shot out to the path and staggered against the steeply rising side of the garden. He was up in an instant—he certainly was fit—but by then she had control of the heavy door, whirling it with all her force to bang shut in his astonished face.

She leant against it for a moment, breathing hard. Then, while Mark hammered and shouted things she didn't want to hear, things muffled by the heavy wood so she needn't listen, she dragged his jacket up by one sleeve. For all she cared he could walk back to the hotel shirt-sleeved and barefoot, but she wanted the place cleansed of him. Trailing the jacket at arm's length, scooping his shoes in her other hand, she climbed the stairs and let herself out to the little balcony off the landing.

'Here,' she called down to where he was still hammering, 'catch!'

He blinked up, surprised by her sudden appearance above him. 'What the. . .? Careful!'

He made a lunge at the jacket, but she had thrown it too wide. It flopped to the grassy slope beyond the path, the contents of its pockets rattling down to the concrete. Mark stooped at once to rescue his personalised lighter, his gold pen, his executive key-ring, and Sally took the chance to drop his shoes. She didn't wait to see where they landed, but hurried inside and bolted the balcony door.

'I'm safe!' she murmured aloud to herself, hardly able to believe it.

In her room, she went straight to the window and closed it. Then she waited like a hidden animal, ready to dodge back into the shadows the minute he should come into sight up the steps.

She needn't have worried. His pale, sinuous figure took them two at a time, without a backward glance, and as soon as it reached the road set off downhill at an angry lope. Presently he disappeared into the distant village street.

Had he really gone? Sally let out a great sigh, and tottered to the bathroom. She completed her bedtime chores by the gentle whiteness of the moon, wanting no other light.

This has to be the end of me and Kingfisher, she

realised as she tumbled against her pillow. And Tara would be the end of me and Kemp, if there'd ever been anything to end.

Images of Kemp and Tara flashed across her mind, sharp as needles. Needles and pins, needles and pins, when a man's married his trouble begins. . .

But they won't, she told herself. She'll be good for him. Try and hang on to that. . .try and hang on. . .try. . .

She pulled the duvet up to her ears, turned her back on the white pain of the moonlight, and fell asleep.

CHAPTER SIX

'Good—morning—Kemp.' Sally slowed her pace thankfully to a halt, dragging in gulps of air. 'I've had—a glorious—jog.'

Well, it had been all right. At least it had taken her mind off her troubles, until the distant sight of the white Mercedes gliding downhill from the castle had brought her almost to a standstill. Even then she'd rallied, and put on her best racing speed for the rise back to the house. She had arrived, spent and gasping, just as Kemp had parked and got out of the car.

He slammed its door. 'You'll do yourself an injury, woman.'

'I didn't—sprint—straight off.' She braced her hands on her knees, resting doubled over while she went on struggling for breath. 'I—warmed up to it—gradually.'

'Suit yourself.'

Why did he sound so very cold and distant? From here she could see only the supple boots, the jeans, the lower hem of the dark blue guernsey sweater. He wouldn't be able to see much of her either, only her lime-green tracksuit and the damp swathes of hair drooping over her face.

Not that I'm hiding from him, she told herself, and went on filling her lungs with the precious, soon-to-be-lost scent of pines and meadows.

The weatherbeaten hands unlocked the luggage section of the Mercedes. 'You've packed, then?'

Did he want so much to be rid of her?

'It won't take me a minute,' she defended herself. 'I've got till five.'

'Wrong.' He raised the cover and hauled out a bright bundle. 'The *plane's* at five. You'll have to leave about two hours——'

'I'll leave now if you want me to.'

'Don't be silly.' He banged the cover shut. 'Can you walk into the house, or have you stiffened up already?'

'Of course I haven't!'

To prove it she straightened, though reluctantly. As she had feared, she couldn't meet his gaze, but dropped hers at once to the cotton bundle he had tucked under his arm. It certainly drew the eyes—a striped confusion of sea-greens and wine-reds and saffrons against the sober blue of his close-knit sweater. Where had she seen those vivid stripes before?

'Come on, then.' He waved her to the steps. 'You won't be able to move tomorrow, but that's your problem.'

Her problem. However much she recoiled from his bluntness, it was the simple truth. Tonight she would sleep in her own flat above the traffic fumes, tomorrow make her way to work—if she still had any work—among the London millions. And if by then she should be aching from having foolishly overstrained herself, he'd never know it. But even if he did, why should he care?

Well, it wouldn't happen.

'I'll be fine,' she asserted. 'I needed the exercise. I've hardly moved since my accident.'

'All the more reason not to go overboard when you do.'

But his voice was distant, impersonal. He wasn't worrying that she might have damaged herself, nor did he mind if she went on damaging herself. He was simply stating a fact.

Sally stared beyond him to the blue-white mountains, remembering all his gentle attention of the past few days. Now it would be for Tara. . . But she wasn't going to think about that.

'After you.' Kemp swept his arm again in that gesture which was part courtesy, part command.

She moved ahead as he meant her to, and found her weary knees already protesting at the effort. Maybe he was right, and she shouldn't have put on that final uphill sprint?

'I didn't go overboard.' She tried to persuade herself it was true. 'It's done me good.' Reaching the front door, she unzipped the breast pocket where she kept her key. 'I feel much better now.'

His feet suddenly pounded the steps above—was he taking them two at a time? Sure enough, before she could look round to check, he had joined her at the door.

'Better than what?'

'Here.' She offered her key, alarmed at this new urgency. 'Let me give you this back, while I think of it.'

He plucked it impatiently from her. 'You needed to feel better. Why?'

'N-no particular reason,' she stammered. 'Or rather. . .' She trailed off, worried by the great shadow looming so close, the height of him between her and the sun. She edged away.

'Come on, tell.' Kemp leant down to her. 'What was making you feel bad?'

'I'll. . . I'll be back in London tomorrow,' she floundered. 'Wouldn't you be depressed at that?'

Had she convinced him? She glanced up to find out,

and realised with a shock that this was the first time
today that she had managed to look directly at him.
Why was the lean jaw so set, the generous mouth so
grim? The blue-grey eyes, diamond-clear in the morning light, drilled into hers.

'So you *are*. . .depressed.' Kemp repeated the word
as if it were the one he had been expecting. 'But only
because you're leaving? No other reason?'

'Well. . .' She stopped. She would most likely be out
of a job soon, but she wasn't about to confide that to
him, not while he looked right into her like this. If she
did, maybe she wouldn't be able to leave it at that.
Maybe she'd find herself going on to speak of the far,
far greater misery of him and Tara. . . 'Isn't it enough?'
she asked.

'It's not the worst thing.'

'It certainly isn't,' she murmured under her breath.

She might have known she wouldn't get away with
it. The cotton bundle flopped to the concrete, the key
jingling beside it as he gripped her shoulder. His other
hand cupped her chin, forcing her to look straight at
him and keep looking.

'You'd better tell me,' he growled with frightening
vehemence. 'It's that louse, isn't it? Has he let you
down already?'

She moved her head in a vain effort to free herself.
'I don't know what you're talking about.'

'You damn well do!' New lines hollowed his cheeks,
narrowed his eyes, pulled his mouth to an unforgiving
line. 'What puzzles me is why you. . .'

He bit off whatever he had been about to say, and
jerked his own head away as if he couldn't bear the
sight of her. Sally pushed at the unyielding thumb on
her shoulder-blade, and squirmed her chin uselessly
from side to side.

'Will you. . .leave me. . .alone?'

He faced towards her again, and glanced from one of his hands to the other as if surprised at what they were doing. Then, with a stony composure that made her feel like a discarded piece of litter, he let her go.

'You d-dropped my key,' she quavered.

She stooped to retrieve it, hardly aware of her own actions, only knowing that she must get away from this new, bewildering distaste he was showing for her. While she fumbled the little toothed metal shape up from the concrete, his voice rasped over her head.

'You might at least have kept him out of my house!'

So that was it. Sally dug the key into her palm, and as she straightened up made a great business of putting it back in her pocket. Her hair had flopped forward again over her hot face, but she left it there, hiding from him now in good earnest.

The silence grew unbearable, and she had to speak. 'H-how did you know?'

'How do you know any tom-cat's been anywhere? They leave their stink.'

Her trembling knees threatened to buckle, and she had to lean against the wall. She closed her eyes. He must be talking about Mark's expensive, spicy after-shave. She could understand anybody disliking that, and it certainly was strong.

'I. . . I didn't notice anything.'

'And if you had,' Kemp's voice bit contemptuously through the swimming red mist behind her eyelids, 'you'd have got rid of it?'

'When. . .?' Sally opened her eyes, and moved her head timidly to indicate the house. 'When were you in there?'

'Last night.' He produced his own key, and opened

the door. 'I came down to make sure you were all right. Which you were.'

'W-was I?'

'Tucked up in bed, and fast asleep after your. . .' He broke off and strode into the hall. She tried blindly to follow, but stumbled over something soft.

'You forgot your. . .whatever it is!' she called after him.

'Dirty washing,' he barked over his shoulder.

So that was where she'd seen this material before. It was the duvet-cover and sheet from his bed at the castle, the same bed he had set her on so gently the evening they'd met.

The bright colours all ran together as she bent towards them. Who had lain on them last night? She picked the bundle up and handed it to him without a word.

'Thanks.' For nothing, his tone implied as he flung it into a corner.

Sally followed him into the living-room, the beautiful innocent room which would never be the same again. The idea somehow made her want to blink, only she wouldn't, wouldn't have tears streaming down her cheeks.

'I'm s-sorry, Kemp. I. . . I didn't mean it to happen—honestly!'

'So he did force you?' He whirled on her, a blurry cyclone of energy. 'My God, I'll——'

'No, no, he didn't.' She wiped her sleeve across her eyes. 'I only meant I'm sorry about. . .' she broke off, not wanting to say the name '. . .about him getting in here. He was—sort of—through the door before I could stop him.'

'He would be.' The cyclone, still blurry, inclined its

head. 'And not too choosy about his methods once he was in, either.'

'Well. . .' She hesitated, wondering how much she dared tell.

'If he didn't force you, he'd have made it damn near impossible for you to refuse. Didn't he?'

She brushed at her eyes a second time, and her vision cleared. Not that it helped much to see his compressed lips, the combative lines of his great shoulders, his white-knuckled fists raised to waist-level.

His gaze, however, was following hers. Just as it had a few minutes ago when he had laid hold of her, it travelled wonderingly from one of his own bunched fists to the other. Slowly he uncurled them, and dropped them to his sides.

His voice stayed urgent. 'You've got to tell me, Sally. I need to know if he. . .how he. . .'

The words seemed to stick in his throat. Sally blinked away the last of her tears and dared to meet the deep-set, diamond-hard eyes. Could he be jealous? But no, he had other reasons, quite understandable reasons, for taking this so seriously.

'You're my guest.' His tone was level now, though jerky and breathless. 'I'm responsible for you.'

'I see.' She felt her whole body droop with something she wouldn't admit was disappointment. 'Well, you hardly need to worry, do you? By this evening——'

'For heaven's sake, stop dodging, woman!' Kemp's hands reached out, and held off a fraction from her shoulders. 'Have I got to shake the truth out of you?'

Sally glanced, as he himself had done earlier, from one of his hands to the other. This really wouldn't do. She straightened her shoulders, and drew herself up as tall as she could.

'You're the one who has to stop,' she rapped out. 'This minute!'

In the electric silence that followed, she only just kept her mouth closed. It wanted to drop open in astonished dismay. Had she really spoken with such authority?

I did, I did, she exulted inwardly, because he might be harming himself. He's got to learn not to take things so hard.

And she held her ground, totally unafraid now between these great, curving hands. Strength flowed back to her knees, her stomach, her spine, and her voice came out cool, steady.

'Now calm down. Try breathing deeply.'

'I need to know how he. . .' Kemp pressed his lips together, and tried again. 'Did he bully you?'

'As you're bullying me now, you mean?'

He frowned at her for a moment longer. Then he took her advice and breathed deeply, his chest expanding and contracting, his breath coming out with a whoosh that lifted the flyaway strands of hair briefly from her forehead. By the time they settled he had turned away from her and was marching over to fling himself into the formal chair by the window.

'Is that better?' he demanded. 'Does that convince you it isn't you I'm threatening?'

I've done it! she rejoiced to herself. I've made him stop, and think about what he's doing, and cool off!

On this victorious surge of sheer delight, all things were possible. Not only possible, but easy. She could see clearly what she had to do, knew exactly the words she had to use.

'I never thought it *was* me you were threatening,' she answered evenly. 'I don't believe you ever could.'

'That's progress, I suppose.' Kemp moved restlessly

within the chair's restraining lines. 'After what you said the night we met.'

'I've learnt a lot about you since then, haven't I?' She smiled, a real smile because she liked the pattern he made over there, all long limbs and insistent vitality penned in by the scrolled wooden armrests. 'You're not a hurter, Kemp, you're a conserver. A helper. A natural——'

'Will you stop this guff,' he broke in with that impatient swatting gesture, 'and tell me what Mark Walsh did to you?'

'All in good time. That is,' she amended, 'if you promise to stay right there, sitting down, until I've finished.'

'Until you've finished, yes,' he agreed grudgingly. 'I can't answer for what I'll do after that.'

'What you won't do is find Mark and beat him to a pulp.'

'I'd thought more of breaking his neck.'

'See?' She looked triumphantly down on him, enjoying the shining swirls of hair at the top of his head which she so seldom had a chance to see. 'You don't mean a word of it.'

'Don't I?' Kemp thumped the scrolled woodwork. 'Just try me.'

'He's the one who'd do that. Or the police.' She paused to let it sink in. 'Criminal assault, I suppose it would be.'

'Criminal assault be damned—it's a service to the human race.' Clearly Kemp saw her argument, but he wasn't persuaded yet. 'If he hurt you, I'll——'

'He didn't,' she assured him hurriedly before he could make any more lurid threats. 'Well, not much, anyway.'

'Any much is too much!' His meaning plain through

the jumbled words, he half rose to his feet. 'Just wait till I——'

'Till you do him a favour?' Sally had raised her voice to be heard. 'Can't you see the mileage he'd get from it?'

Clearly, he could. He thrust his hands deep in his pockets, and reluctantly dropped back into his seat.

'"KEMP WHITTAKER IN PUNCH-UP",' Sally quoted the imaginary headline. 'Why, it might even make the quality papers. Mark would certainly do his best to see it did.'

'Hell and damnation!'

'"All publicity's good publicity",' she quoted mercilessly. 'I've heard him say it often.'

'Isn't he supposed to be running a high-class outfit?'

'Just now, yes, but who knows what he'll be wanting to do in a year or two? "The bigger the name",' she quoted another of Mark's often-repeated maxims, '"the bigger the enterprise".'

'The bigger the pile of. . .' He left the comment unfinished. 'Look, I'm not interested in the career of this. . .' He broke off again, baffled. 'I can't think of a single term that's fit to be heard by a lady.'

'So I'm a lady, am I?' Sally felt a bubble of laughter rising within her. 'Oh, Kemp, you're so. . .'

Now it was her turn to stop, choking back the word she'd been about to use. 'So lovable', she'd wanted to say, and it wasn't easy to find anything to put in its place.

'So old-fashioned.' It was the best she could manage.

'If it's old-fashioned to want to know what goes on under my own roof,' growled Kemp, 'then that's what I am. Get on with it, woman. What did he do to you?'

'Nothing much.' She took a chair on the other side of the low table and cast her mind over last night's events, trying to put them in order. 'There wasn't time, really.'

'So he didn't. . . I mean, you're still. . .'

'Still a virgin, yes.'

Another wall-shaking sigh escaped him. She could almost see the pent-up aggression leaving with it, the muscles relaxing, the arms straightening and easing along the chair-arms, the swirling hair settling against the swirling woodwork of the backrest.

'I wish you wouldn't keep on about my. . .my inexperience,' she went on tartly. 'As you said yourself when we met this morning, that's my problem.'

'I didn't say it about this.' Kemp shot her a glance. 'I hate to think of that toad with. . .anybody decent.'

Like Tara, for instance? Had that girlish sweetness already roused the protective instinct which was so much a part of Kemp Whittaker's nature? Had she been telling him. . .? But no, Sally couldn't bear to imagine anything that might have taken place last night between Tara and Kemp.

'Well, you don't have to,' she snapped to cover her pain. 'Or not with me, anyway.'

'But how on earth. . .what did you. . .?' Kemp broke off in frustration at not being able to speak his mind. 'Dammit, Sally, he must have chased you all over the house!'

Sally let out a nervous giggle at the absurdity. 'He wasn't here long enough for that. I—er——' she looked down at her own hands, vaguely surprised at their slenderness '—it was the moon, really. And needing some air.'

'You're not making sense.' But Kemp was coherent himself now, and willing to piece the story together as she gave it. 'What I want to know is how you got rid of him,' he explained. 'Mark Walsh sure as hell wouldn't go till he was pushed.'

'That's it.' Sally leant forward, glad to have been given a starting point. 'I pushed him. Out of the door.'

'And he stood there and let you?'

'I did, honestly,' she assured him, sensitive to his disbelief. 'I opened the door to. . .' She trailed off, not wanting to speak of her near-consent and later revulsion. 'To look at the moon,' she finished in a rush.

He frowned. 'Why were you doing anything so romantic?'

'Only pretending.'

'I'd rather you hadn't pretended anything, with that skunk.'

'And what else was I to do? Where. . .?' She broke off, biting her tongue to silence. 'Where were you?' That was what she'd wanted to ask, but she couldn't, it was none of her business. Anyway, she knew the answer. She gazed at the bundle of bed-linen and the last of her elation seeped away, leaving her stranded with the cold, solid facts.

Drearily, she summoned them to the job in hand. 'I couldn't throw him out by the scruff of the neck and the seat of his pants, could I?'

'No,' he agreed on a note of longing. 'I see that. So you opened the door. And he came out to look at the moon with you?'

'Do you really think he'd ever do that?'

In the new, cold light of her reasoning, she could even meet those diamond-hard eyes. And they weren't hard any more, but alight with a warmth and interest only briefly shadowed with dislike as he worked out the answer to her question.

'Mark Walsh wouldn't be bothered,' he agreed. 'So how did you get him to the door?'

'He wanted to. . .' Sally paused, aware of the blush rising in her cheeks. 'He thought I was wasting time. So he sort of—shouldered me inside, so he could shut the door.'

'Mmm.' He nodded, tight-lipped. 'That figures.'

'After that, all I had to do was get behind him, and push.'

'Just. . .push?' he repeated, savouring the word.

'And bang the door before he——'

But she couldn't go on—her voice had drowned in his great shout of delight. She waited stonily, but he wasn't with her at all. He'd flung his head back, his sturdy throat rippling with laughter, his dark mane tangled across the curlicues of the chair, his splendid teeth all on display. Completely off guard like this he looked more dangerous than ever, like a forest wolf full-fed and playful after a kill.

Presently he dug into his pocket and fished out a huge red and white striped handkerchief. Something came with it, another strip of material, brighter but smoother, which he threw down between them.

'So that's how you knew Mark was here!' She stared at the flame-coloured silk uncurling on the table. 'I thought you'd smelt his aftershave.'

'I did.'

Kemp's mouth pulled in again, and she realised it expressed more than mere dislike. What she read in his eyes was downright aversion, a hatred for Mark Walsh and all his ilk and all their works.

And that included me, when he thought I'd. . . She felt her own mouth tighten as she remembered how very close she had come to accepting Mark as her lover.

And even though I didn't, she realised in despair, it's Mark's world I belong in, not Kemp's.

Trying to blot out the misery of it, she indicated the tie, a flame-coloured snake between the bowl of fruit and the vase of flowers. 'He took it off at the party.'

'Did he? I didn't notice.'

'No—well, it was about the time Tara stepped out of her shoes.' Sally tried not to sound bitter, though the words were like vinegar in her mouth. 'Where did you find it?'

'Out there.' Kemp gestured at the hall. 'On the stairs.'

'I s-see.' She stumbled on the simple phrase. 'No wonder you thought——'

'I'm surprised I didn't wake you the minute I found it,' he cut in as if he didn't want to hear more. 'The first thing I did was tear up to your room.'

His room, she silently corrected him. He'd slept there before he moved to the castle, and the whole space breathed of him. Each time she rose on tiptoe before the tiny glass to comb her hair, she was reminded of his height and his lack of vanity. The tall, luxuriously carved chest of drawers and wardrobe were full of his scent. As for the solid pine double bed— how could she even have dreamt of letting Mark into that?

'Yes, well, I'm sorry.' Kemp had noted her shudder. 'But at least I let you sleep, once I saw he wasn't in there with you.'

'Don't!' She hated to think of it, hated to think how nearly it had happened, yet had to know more. 'What would you have done if he had been?'

'Gone away, and had the place fumigated later. Or so I'd like to believe.' He hesitated. 'You can see, can't you, that even though you were alone by then, I didn't know if——?'

'You were still furious,' she broke in, sympathising. 'Just to know he'd been here, in your house.'

'It wasn't only. . . Well, never mind.' He hurried on, 'I wanted to have it out with you then and there.'

'Why didn't you?'

'I don't know. You were sleeping so peacefully. . .' He brushed the subject aside with a sharp motion of his hand in the direction of the tie. 'How did it get on the stairs?'

'It must have fallen out of his pocket.' She recalled with satisfaction how she had trailed the jacket upstairs by one sleeve. 'I wasn't very careful with his things when I carried them up to throw from the balcony.'

'You what?' The volcanic laughter sparked once more from his eyes, rumbled once more in his chest.

'I'm glad you're amused,' she said coldly. 'It didn't seem funny at the time.'

'No.' He tried to be serious. 'I'd have got here sooner, but. . .' He broke off, the laugh rumbling to another full-throated explosion. 'Some people get roses. . .thrown to them. . .from balconies,' he gasped when he could speak. 'Mark Walsh gets. . .his clothes!'

'Only his jacket and shoes,' Sally corrected.

That set him off again, but he quickly caught her eye and dabbed the striped handkerchief to his own. When he had finished mopping, he stuffed the handkerchief away in his pocket and leant forward to pick up the tie. He handled it without the slightest reluctance, Sally noted with relief. Somehow the poison had all gone from it, drained away by her ridiculous story and his healthy enjoyment of it.

'He really meant business, did he?'

'He did.'

'You showed him, though.' Kemp flicked the flame-coloured length of silk like a whip.

'You might say so,' she agreed frostily. 'And tomorrow morning he'll be showing me right back.'

'Tell me.' He stopped playing with the tie and surveyed her with his shaggy head on one side, all attention.

'Nothing much to tell. Especially about the Kingfisher account.' Sally stared through the open window at the wide, clean skies which were to be hers for such a little time longer. 'Would you want your publicity handled by a woman who'd thrown you out, and your clothes after you?'

As if any woman would need to, she added to herself, or ever, ever want to.

'You surely don't intend to go on working with him after this?'

Sally blinked, and realised she'd been staring into the clear-sighted eyes with a hunger which was almost physical. She shook her head in confusion.

'Of course not. But I do need to go on working.'

Kemp flung down the tie, so forcefully that the limp object skidded across the table and landed at Sally's feet. 'You must have some less repulsive customers?'

'Not enough. And those I did have. . .'

But she wasn't going into all that. How Tara, sweetly murmuring about 'easing the pressure on you', had dealt more and more with the other accounts, until the Silk people automatically asked for her, and the producer of the Lantern commercials had invited her to their latest filming.

And why did I let that happen? Sally demanded of herself. Because I was slaving for Mark, that's why. She toed the flame-coloured silk aside with one leaf-mould-speckled trainer. I must have been mad!

Aloud, she admitted the stark, cold truth.

'If. . .*when* I lose Kingfisher, they'll fire me from Limelight.'

'And that's bad?'

She glanced up sharply, ready to counter a new attack on her job. But Kemp's eyes were gentle, and the frown between his brows showed nothing but concern and sympathy. Whatever he thought of her work, he was taking her problem seriously.

'It paid the rent,' she told him with a sigh. 'And it was more interesting than lots of other things I could have been doing.'

'I see.' And he did. 'You're saying you could get another job easily enough, but it would be less. . .' He broke off, then with a visible effort kept strictly to her point of view. 'Less responsible, and less well paid.'

She nodded. 'I can go back easily enough to typing, putting stuff in computers, pushing paper about.' She looked ahead, the sunny morning blotted out by memories of those early days in Limelight. 'It's taken me five years to work up from that.'

'And you really have to start again?' He shifted in his chair, searching for solutions. 'You couldn't persuade another agency to take you at the same level you are now?'

'After the mess I've made of things here?' She kept her voice even, wanting him to know she wasn't blaming him for it any more. 'If a job was going, nobody would look at me.'

For a moment longer Kemp sat in silence, arched brows drawn together, generous mouth pursed in thought. Then he sat up with a sudden resolve.

'Right.' The frown had gone, and the narrowed eyes now gleamed with predatory zest, the wolf scenting prey. 'We'd better make sure you keep this one.'

'Oh, yes?' Sally eyed him cynically, refusing to join

in his enthusiasm. 'And then we'll find a mare's nest, and have the eggs for lunch.'

'Lunch!' He sprang to his feet. 'Had you forgotten we've got an invitation? You'd better change.'

She stared up at him, incredulous. 'You can't intend to go down there and *eat* with Mark?' she gasped.

'I think I can bring myself to.' He shot her a wicked sideways look. 'In the circumstances.'

'But after what I did to him last night——'

'Those are the circumstances.'

'But, Kemp, he won't want to see me, let alone feed me.'

'That's right. What we're going to watch——' Kemp flung his arms above his head and stretched to his full length, an enormous figure of unholy glee '—is Mark Walsh having to be hospitable to a woman who's turned him down flat.'

'I see.' Sally straightened in her chair with a fury made all the worse by the way she was having to crane up at him. 'You want to rub it in that he's been made a fool of, and I'm to be the. . .the rubber!'

She bit her lip, more annoyed than ever that it had come out so silly. Kemp, however, had already sauntered to the dining-table to lift the phone from its corner ledge.

'Of course I'll enjoy making Walsh behave decently to you,' he agreed with relish. 'But that's only a nice little extra. The objective's your job. Seeing as you're so keen.'

Sally twisted uncomfortably in her chair to watch him at the other side of the room. 'And I keep Mark's account by inflicting my company on him for lunch?'

But he was already speaking into the phone, asking for Mr Walsh and giving his own name. Waiting to be put through, he grinned at her.

'What's the betting your Casanova won't be available?'

'To you?' she asked, bewildered. 'Of course he will.'

'Not if he thinks I've heard about what went on here last night. Ah, Tara.'

Sally felt her stomach churn. So this was his real reason for taking up the invitation—the chance to see Tara again. Look at him now—triumphant grin softened to a caressing smile.

'Dear me, how disappointing.' He shot Sally an I-told-you-so glance, but his language and voice were mellow as she had never known them. 'So where do we stand on this business of my name on the brochures, then?'

Sally sat bolt upright. 'You'd do that?'

'Sure, sure,' he soothed into the phone, and waited. The wicked triumph returned in all its force as he glanced across to Sally. 'That's fetched him.'

She sprang to her feet and hurried to the table. 'You'd really agree to it?'

'Hi, Walsh.' Kemp's voice became brisk and laconic. 'So when shall we show? Yes, of course Sally'll be with me. You asked her, didn't you?'

The voice at the other end of the line might have been objecting.

'Packing won't take a minute,' Kemp pointed out. 'We can't upset the deal for that.' He cocked his head, listening to a suggestion on the other end of the line. 'With Tara, you mean?'

'You see?' Sally slumped in despair to the other corner-bench. 'He's already——'

She broke off in incredulous dismay. Kemp wasn't just considering the idea, he was liking it. She could tell by the fond light in his eyes, the cherishing tenderness which Tara's golden fragility brought out in so many men.

'It'll certainly be nice to have her there,' he agreed. 'But—er——' he paused significantly '—three's a crowd, Walsh. You wouldn't want to play gooseberry, would you?'

'Neither would I!' Sally muttered from the other side of the table.

Kemp swatted her to silence. 'Besides, it's still officially Sally's account.'

'It is for now,' she mouthed cynically. 'Until. . .'

Until as long as it took her pretty junior to wrap this great, guileless, gentlemanly goof round her little finger. Sally scrambled up from the bench.

'I won't go,' she announced, and hurried from the room.

CHAPTER SEVEN

'DON'T bother to knock,' Sally observed sarcastically from where she stood on the heavy alpine chair.

'What's the point of knocking when the door's wide open?' Kemp hurried round the bed. 'Let me do that.'

'No, thanks.'

She returned stubbornly to her task. It was proving trickier than she had allowed for, reaching up over the chair's heart-shaped back to bring down her suitcase from the wardrobe top. On no account must she damage the lovingly carved frieze of doves along its upper edge, so she had to balance the suitcase high and wide before she could lower it. Too high and too wide for her strength, she had just begun to realise when Kemp had charged in as if he owned the place.

'I don't know why you put it up here at all,' she grumbled, remembering how easily he'd raised it to this height five days ago. 'There's plenty of room inside the cupboard.'

'If you'll just get down off this chair——'

'Stop crowding me! How can I work out the best way to do it with you hovering like that?'

'This is the best way to do it,' Kemp said firmly.

He stretched an arm past her and lifted the suitcase, so lightly that it might have grown wings. She watched it soar over the courting birds and settle on the floor below her feet.

'I'd have managed, if you'd let me. I'm not completely helpless!'

'Maybe not.' He regarded her coolly from under the

125

arched brows. 'But you certainly can be an ungracious little tyke.'

'Will you stop badgering me? I need to get on with my packing.'

'You need your job—or so I understood.'

Sally bit her lip. How to explain that the price was too high? That she couldn't bear to sit at the same table with him and Tara, knowing what she knew about them?

'So perhaps,' he insisted, 'you'll tell me why you flounced out just now.'

'I did not flounce!'

'You flounced. Leaving me stuck with a deal I fixed entirely on your behalf.'

'I don't want your deals, thank you.'

'Right.'

The single word rumbled from his throat like thunder, but she had no time to be frightened by it. Her waist was seized by two warm hands, the sunny room whirled, and her feet landed on the floorboards. She staggered, swayed, caught for balance at the blue sweater, and came to rest leaning against the broad shoulder beneath it.

'You don't want my deals.' The hands stayed at her waist, steadying her. 'And you think I fixed this for the pleasure of the company?'

She vainly tried to break free. 'I know why you fixed it!'

'Good.' Only one of his hands pinioned her, the other tilting her face up to his. 'Then I don't have to tell you.'

She couldn't struggle any more. Her arms simply wouldn't obey her will, but stole of their own accord round his neck while her lips melted to his. It was the tenderest of kisses, making no demands on her, the hard mouth content to stay close to hers until she should choose where they were to go from here.

But she had no choice. Her lips had to part and let him in, her tongue to lap at his, her fingers to glory in his tangled hair, her body to nestle against his hard sinews which she so much wanted to be hers, forever hers against the world.

Only when she felt the surge of his masculine desire did she draw back, dropping her arms from about his neck. 'It doesn't mean a thing, does it?'

'What doesn't?' He let her go, but his steely gentleness hinted at the physical frustration he was keeping in control.

'Th-that.' She showed her meaning with a brief gesture, and looked away, cheeks flaming. 'Men have those like. . .like women have babies. I mean,' she added hastily, determined to explain herself, 'it's just something your body gets on with, whatever the rest of you——'

'I'm with you,' he cut in, dry and cold as hailstones. 'And you, of course, are an expert on the subject.'

'That's not fair!' She faced him, wide-eyed. 'Just because I'm. . .just because I haven't. . .'

'It's me we're talking about.' The hailstones pelted remorselessly. 'You seem to think you know all about me. That you can read my mind.'

'Not your m-mind,' she stammered, determined to get it out. 'Your b-body. Th-the t-two aren't the same, are they?'

'Sometimes they are. Sometimes not.'

His eyes had shuttered, revealing nothing, yet answering the question she hadn't dared ask. Telling her she had no place in his mind, his home, his heart. That his healthy male sexuality was the only part of him involved with her. As if to confirm it, he carried the suitcase to the bed, opened it, and stood back, inviting her to pack and get out of his life.

'As I said, it doesn't mean a thing,' she railed, overcome by a savage desire to hurt him. 'Any more than it did with Mark.'

'Wait a minute!' Kemp whipped round to stare at her, quiet but deadly. 'Do I understand you're comparing me with Walsh?'

'You're both men, aren't you?' Carefully not looking at him, Sally moved to the chest of drawers.

He flashed across the room to confront her. 'So that's how much you've learnt about me in five days?'

She quailed, reminded how terrifying he could be. Fiery-eyed, icy-lipped, hair still thrashing in the wind of his passage, he might have been a tree-spirit rising to avenge an insult. And it *had* been an insult and worse, she realised, obscurely ashamed. He and Mark were different as oak and mistletoe, different root, stock, and branch.

'I. . . I'm not saying you're like him in other ways,' she admitted, hating herself for having ever mentioned the loathed name.

Perhaps he saw how he had frightened her. The fire left him, the ice melted, the wind settled, and he was once more the rangy, approachable human being she had come to depend on. Except, she reminded herself harshly, that she mustn't ever let herself do that. She hadn't the right.

As if to confirm it, Kemp dismissed her and her opinions with the familiar swatting gesture. 'You've accepted an obligation, and you're meeting it.' His voice dropped to a flinty command. 'Get changed.'

Sally's courage returned as she bristled at the curt order. However imperious, however abrupt, he was a man again, and no man had any right to tell her what to do.

'I will,' she snapped. 'In my own good time.'

'You'll do it now.'

'Are you going to make me?'

'If I have to.' He came closer, much too close, and grabbed the welt of her tracksuit top in both hands. 'Shall we start with your shower?'

Sally stared down at the bunched lime-green fabric. Beneath it her heart pounded, her breasts rose and fell, the skin of her waist burned and chilled, chilled and burned at the brush of his knuckles.

'Though we might be a bit delayed——' his silky murmur was almost to himself '—once I've taken your clothes off.'

'You wouldn't!'

'Wouldn't I? All men are the same, aren't they?'

'But n-not like this,' she pleaded, knowing how much she was in his power, how little she could resist his lovemaking if he chose to ignore her protests. 'Not like this, Kemp!'

'So you understand that much.' He released her, opened the single drawer which was all she had needed for her clothes, and took out her sleeveless black T-shirt. 'This should be formal enough.'

She accepted the sombre garment. 'I was planning to wear that anyway—for the plane journey.'

'Good, then you won't need to change again before you leave.'

'I won't, will I?'

The fight had drained out of her. He spoke so lightly of her leaving, and why not? His life here would go on, his work at the castle and his leisure in the forest and the village. If any of that changed, it wouldn't be her doing.

Not hers. She'd be somewhere else, hunting for a new job or getting on with this one Kemp was trying to save for her. Yes, he was right, it was for her he'd organised this, not for himself.

'I'm sorry, Kemp.' She hung her head.

The long, muscular fingers touched her cheek, light as a falling leaf and as quickly gone. 'Friends?' he queried.

She nodded, not trusting herself to speak. If friendship was what he offered, then she must accept it and think herself lucky.

She held on to the thought later, as they walked down to the hotel. Her shower had refreshed her briefly, but now the May sunlight stroked her bare arms to drugged heaviness, and she knew Kemp had been right about that uphill sprint at the end of her jog this morning. She shouldn't have done it.

Well, tomorrow would be when she'd really pay for it, so he would never know. All she had to do now was keep her wits about her, and get through this unbearable occasion with as much dignity as possible.

Her determination was tested as soon as they entered the hotel's wide, quiet lobby. A few guests murmured here and there on the scattered chairs and couches, but none of them was Mark. Had he changed his mind after all? Had he decided he wouldn't meet her again, even with the lure of Kemp for publicity?

Or was she worrying too soon? At any rate, here was Tara, coming out of the archway that led to the restaurant. They met by the mahogany flower table, which today held a porcelain oyster-shell opening on a luxuriance of apple blossom and iris.

'Kemp, darling!' Tara put her hands on his shoulders, rose on tiptoe, and kissed his cheek. Sally watched miserably, but presently had to submit to a similar, delicately perfumed welcome.

'Mark's in there.' Tara nodded towards the restaurant. 'Why don't you join him, Kemp, while we go to the powder-room,' she caught Sally's eye, 'for some girl talk?'

'You do that,' urged Kemp. 'Then I can. . .' He broke off and corrected himself, mouth quirking. 'Then *we* can *both* look forward to—er—to seeing you again.'

Sally knew exactly what he meant. Tara, blue flowered silk drifting and whispering round her, was as much a feast for the eyes as ever, but that wasn't what he'd be waiting for. The event he would look forward to was Mark's reaction to her own arrival. If he were already seated at the table while she approached from the entrance, he'd be able to enjoy it all the more.

The ghoul! she fumed inside. He might remember how rotten it's going to be for me!

At least she could put it off, she decided, and deliberately slowed her walk across the blond parquet. Not till they had reached the lavender-carpeted Ladies' room did she remember that meaning glance which had summoned her here.

'Girl talk?' She repeated the phrase with some distaste. 'Have you something to tell me?'

'Not exactly.' Tara stared critically at her reflection in the mirror above the washbasins, brought a neat little make-up pouch from her neat little handbag, and extracted an eyelash-brush. 'Mark's in a mood, but I expect you knew that already.'

Sally felt the pink rising in her own cheeks. 'And you're wondering why?'

'I can guess.' Tara brushed at one dark eyebrow, then the other. 'Unwise, darling,' she added, returning the little brush to its pouch. 'That man's a career breaker if ever I saw one.'

'Don't you do your lashes?' Sally stared at the heavy, unlikely black fringes. 'Or might they come unstuck?'

The eyelashes fanned upwards. 'That's not like you, Sally.'

'It isn't, is it?' Sally agreed, wondering at herself. 'Maybe I'm just sick of every kind of fake.'

'They won't come unstuck. Nothing about me ever does.' The caressing voice sharpened, showing its iron undertones. 'And it's high time you learnt a bit of faking yourself.'

Sally glanced in the mirror, and saw her own chin set to a stubborn little square. 'I've managed without it so far.'

'Have you?' The light laugh was edged with malice. 'You think those advertising slogans of yours were all, always, absolutely true?'

'I never lied about a product.'

'Come on, darling, it's only a matter of how far you're prepared to go.' Tara unsheathed her lipstick. 'Which brings us right back to Mark Walsh.'

'Does it?' Sally turned on the cold tap.

'Believe me, I know how you feel,' Tara told her.

Sally glanced up, caught by the change of tone. Could that be genuine sympathy in the carefully soft voice? She wasn't sure. Her assistant was three years younger than herself, and looked younger still, yet the iris-blue eyes held an ancient shrewdness, a street wisdom old as womankind.

'I've been there,' Tara confirmed. 'All the way. And pretended I enjoyed it.'

'Though you didn't?' Sally couldn't resist asking.

'I often wonder about that sort of man.' Tara manipulated her gold tube of lipstick, its pink column

slowly rising. 'I don't think it's sex they're after at all.
I think what turns them on is power.'

'The power of the stoat over the rabbit,' Sally
murmured under the clean rushing sound of the water.

She remembered the detail which had finally
prompted her desperate action against Mark. She
hadn't been hoping for much pleasure—it was the
small, carelessly inflicted pain which had repelled her,
and his casual assurance that she'd get used to it. She
held her hands under the running tap, and spoke
louder.

'Do you mean you've. . .been with. . .lots like him?'

'The woods are full of them.' Tara freshened up the
rosy outline of her mouth. 'If a woman wants to get
anywhere, she goes along with them.'

'You shouldn't.' Sally washed her hands more thor-
oughly than she ever had in her life. 'It's wrong.'

'That's how things are.' The lipstick vanished into
the pouch. 'Who are we to change it? He's still after
you.' The blue eyes studied their two images, the
brown and black and the blue and gold, with open
curiosity. 'Goodness knows why.'

Sally rinsed off soap. 'Because he hasn't caught me
yet?'

'I thought that might be it!' said Tara triumphantly.
'So for goodness' sake let him.'

Sally looked up, and saw real concern in the mirrored
eyes. This woman, she realised with harsh amusement,
was giving what she saw as serious advice, from the
ugly depths of her own experience.

'So that's what you brought me here to say?' she
queried.

'Be sensible, darling! It only needs a bit of
flattery. . .'

'Thank you, Grandma, but I'd sooner suck eggs!'

Tara shrugged, giving up. 'Then you'd better find another business to work in.'

'We'll see. I'm here, aren't I?' Sally turned off the tap, pressed the knob of the drying machine, and raised her voice to be heard over it. 'And still running the account, as far as I know.'

'Not for long. You're only here because Kemp wouldn't come without you, the high-minded hunk.' The blue eyes took on a frosty, starry glint. 'He won't be doing much more of that kind of thing.'

Sally concentrated on shaking the wet off her hands. 'You sound very sure.'

'I am.' The unfaltering coo pierced the drier's hot wind like a shower of iron darts. 'Kemp Whittaker's mine, darling.'

'After one meeting?'

'One meeting's enough, when you know your stuff. What you could have done with five days!' Tara marvelled. 'Luckily for me, you're as innocent as he is.'

'Innocent?' Sally swallowed, dry-throated. 'So that's how you see us.'

'Mm,' Tara nodded. 'Only he's gorgeous with it. And rich, and famous. Just my dish.'

'Your *what*? No, don't say it again,' Sally held up a damp hand. 'You're nothing but a female Mark!'

'Jealous, darling? I can understand that.' A cream-fed smile hovered at the pink-painted mouth. 'Take my word for it, I won't have to fake when Kemp makes love to me.'

'Love?' Sally echoed in a fury. 'I don't believe you know what it means!'

'Oh, yes, I do.' Tara settled a curl with satisfied fingers. 'It means getting that little gold band through his nose, so you can lead him where he should go.'

'Ugh! And where, in your opinion, should Kemp Whittaker go?'

'Back to real life, of course. A proper home in London, another in Paris, or New York, or both. Receptions.' Tara gazed at her starry, frosty reflection. 'You have to see the right people. I'll be Lady Whittaker before I'm done.'

'And to think I believed. . .' Sally broke off, the words dying in her throat. 'I believed you'd be *good* for Kemp' would have sounded just too silly to this predatory little creature. 'I don't care if you're the Grand Duchess of Fandango,' she used instead her mother's homely phrase. 'Kemp won't be along. He hates the thing you call,' she paused with distaste, '"real life".'

'You mean he doesn't know what's good for him.' Tara turned to the door. 'Just watch me teach him!'

'So this is why you're being so generous with the advice about keeping Mark happy!' Sally hissed as the door swung shut after them. 'Because you're after bigger game.'

'Don't be unkind, darling.' The little mouth, dawn pink in the airy sunshine of the corridor, formed a brief, angelic pout. 'I never meant to hang about at Limelight anyway.'

'So you've always been on the look-out for a——'

'For the right guy—aren't we all? Only some of us have a better idea how to set about it.' They reached the hotel lobby, and Tara fixed her public smile in place. 'I was only offering a word to the wise.'

'That's not wisdom.' Sally padded in her trainers beside the tapping high heels. 'It's. . .it's *pandering*!'

'Don't exaggerate, darling.' Tara paused at the arch-way to the restaurant. 'Mark may not be perfect, but you were keen on him once, and no wonder. Just look at him!'

Sally did. How could she not? Every woman in the comfortably busy restaurant must be aware of the two men at the table by the window, each in his way so strikingly handsome. Mark's hair shone gold in the sunlight, his icy green tie harmonised perfectly with his eyes, his light suit showed its fine tailoring with every flexible movement. By contrast Kemp, shaggy-haired and large-limbed in the dark blue sweater, seemed more than ever built for outdoors, too big and rough for the crystal and silver and starched white linen around him.

Yet he dominated without even trying. Look at Mark deferring to him, eagerly explaining, hoping to win him over. And Kemp was leaning back, open, relaxed, one elbow on the windowsill, head turned to gaze out to the slopes of the distant forest.

He'd rather be anywhere but here, with us, Sally thought on an unbearable surge of longing. He's too real for all of us. A man of truth. . .

'Seeing them like this,' Tara's iron coo was almost a welcome distraction, 'makes me realise how much work needs doing on Kemp.'

'What it makes me realise. . .' Sally trailed off, pushing at the strap of the sensible handbag she had brought with her five days ago. Aeons ago, as it seemed at this moment. When she had chosen this bag for travelling, she had seen Mark as a dream lover. Now he just looked dream-trivial—lightweight, a fantasy melting in the sun. 'I don't like men who've been worked on,' she finished, unable to put it any more clearly.

'I know what you mean, darling,' said Tara, though she obviously didn't. 'I love a challenge myself.'

'You'll never turn a Kemp Whittaker into a Mark Walsh.'

'Heaven forbid!' Tara smiled like a spring morning, and floated forward in her blossom-white and blue-flowered silk. 'I'm after something much better than that.'

Sally reluctantly followed, stiffening against the ordeal to come. Would Mark be openly hostile, or would he hold back until he'd got what he wanted? And, for that matter, what did he want? If Tara had spoken the truth, then last night's rejection had only whetted his appetite. Sally shuddered.

But I needn't go along with it, she reminded herself. I'd sooner lose his account. I'd sooner scrub floors for a living than be as. . .as contemptible as he is!

Only he didn't look in the least contemptible. Far from it; the turn of his head as they approached was composed, elegant, formidable. One glance in her direction, so fleeting she might have imagined it, and he was all courteous host.

It was Kemp who changed with their arrival. He immediately sat straighter, and if he was disappointed by Mark's confident greeting he didn't show it. His eyes lit up, and he rose at once to greet them across the table's centrepiece of wreathed anemones.

'I thought you were never coming.'

'All beautiful, then?' Mark had risen more slowly, merely to conform with his guest's old-fashioned code, but he eyed Tara approvingly. 'I can see it was worth waiting for.'

'Neither of you looks any different to me.' Kemp's gaze flashed from one to the other. 'But I'm still glad to see you.'

Mark shot him a brief, veiled glance, then busied himself with the seating arrangements. 'What about the beefsteak?' he suggested when they were all supplied with leather-bound menus. 'Kemp says it comes from the farm down the road.'

'Everything else does too,' Kemp pointed out impassively. 'The Herdis farm organically,' he added to Sally, knowing she would recognise the name and the land. 'Their cattle win prizes.'

'Steak it is, then,' she agreed.

'And for starters?' Mark asked her.

'None for me.' She tried to copy his cool politeness. 'I can only ever manage one thing at a time.'

'I'll make a note of that.'

Sally looked up in alarm. Did the comment carry a hidden barb? She couldn't tell; the green eyes were already engaged elsewhere, and full of a satisfaction she would rather not have understood.

'Caviare, flowerpuss?'

'Marvellous, darling!' Tara responded with a private purr. 'How clever of you, to remember my favourite thing!'

'Just as you like, of course,' Kemp's voice tore through the moment of intimacy. 'But it'll be out of a jar.'

Could he be jealous? Tara, fluttering the stuck-on lashes to superb effect, made it quite clear he had no need to be.

'What would *you* recommend?' she asked him.

'The trout's good.' Kemp pointed to it on the menu. 'They fetch it daily from the valley.'

'I'll have it,' Tara agreed swiftly. '*Meunière*, please, Mark, instead of the steak.'

'You'll want a white with that.' Mark turned his menu to the wine list. 'What about a Pouilly Fuissé?'

'They do a very good local white by the carafe,' Kemp announced flatly.

Mark's smile thinned a little. 'And that's what you'd prefer for yourself?'

'Thank you, I never drink at midday.'

Was the abruptness deliberate, or an instinctive reaction to their host's suave veneer? Sally refused wine in her turn, and thought crossly that, since Kemp had made her come here, he might try a bit harder.

Tara, too, decided to follow his lead, and drink water. 'We do have a plane to catch,' she reminded Mark, and immediately gave Kemp the full force of her black-fringed, iris-blue eyes. 'Tell me about the owl chicks. Are you doing a programme on them?'

'Next year, maybe,' he answered, animated for the first time since the moment of their arrival. 'If they grow up and breed. They're getting quite big now. . .'

'I want a word with you on your own, when we've finished here.' Mark laid a well-manicured hand on Sally's arm.

She tried, and failed, to move it away. 'What's to be said?' she asked him.

'Quite a lot. I've got plans for you, Sal.'

'Plans?' Knowing the relentless egotism beneath the surface charm, she began to understand Kemp's contrariness. 'Well, I've none that involves you!'

'I hope you've some that involve my account, though.'

'I'm to keep it?' She hesitated, not knowing whether to believe him or not. 'After everything that's happened. . .'

'I'll level with you,' he interrupted smoothly. 'I did intend to pass it on to Tara. But—well. . .' He nodded at the other two '. . .need I say more?'

He needn't. Kemp, coaxed into his favourite topic of the moment, was feeling in one of his pockets after another. 'I could show you the construction better if I drew it,' he told Tara.

'Here.' The little bag clicked open to produce a gold-tooled Filofax and a gold pencil. 'I'll have the drawing as a keepsake.'

Kemp laughed, and accepted the offerings. While he sketched the hide from which he observed his owls, Tara's pink filbert nails played against his wrist.

Unable to watch any longer, Sally turned back to Mark. He couldn't do much to her if they stayed firmly here in the dining-room, she decided, and he was the key to her job for the moment. She had to have a future of some kind. There had to be something to fill this new, dragging emptiness at the centre of her being.

If I can only get Limelight to keep me on, I'll go full out on my other accounts, she promised herself. And get new ones. No more eggs in one basket for me, especially this basket!

'OK,' she agreed, cool now as Mark himself. 'We'll talk here, over coffee, shall we?'

After that, everything went more easily. The white-gloved waiter set their choices before them on silver chafing-dishes, dealt out plates too hot to touch, and skilfully filleted Tara's trout. The three lavish steaks parted like butter to the knives, and Sally was sure she could taste in hers the wild-flower freshness of the alpine meadows. Or maybe it was just the rich juices of the meat itself. At any rate, the tiny new potatoes and simply dressed green salad set it off to perfection. For a blessed interlude, all was peace and tinkling silverware. The peace continued, strained but holding, while Kemp demolished a gigantic portion of cherry tart and the rest of them toyed with gruyère cheese.

'Now, Kemp,' said Mark as the last plates were cleared, 'what about that endorsement?'

Kemp turned to Sally in unspoken question. She gazed back at him imploringly, and he sighed.

'I've talked to the manager here.' He nodded round the quietly luxurious room. 'They'd like the business, naturally, so I'd be doing them a favour.'

'You'd be doing yourself one.' Mark named a sum that took Sally's breath away.

Not Kemp's though. 'That, of course, is without photo?'

Mark's eyelids flickered, and he expanded into the wheeler-dealer territory he understood. 'As long as it's our photo, specially taken.' He named another sum.

'Delivered when?' Kemp demanded.

'On signature.'

'I sign nothing,' Kemp said firmly.

Mark barely wavered. 'Then at a time to be stated.'

'In writing.'

'I'll see to it. And now,' Mark glanced at his watch, 'we've time for Tara to go up to the castle with you——'

'No!' Sally and Kemp spoke together.

'Not the castle,' Kemp affirmed.

'We'll use the farmhouse.' Sally wouldn't look in Tara's direction. 'And *I'll* supervise the photo session.'

'Eventually, yes,' Mark agreed calmly, organisation man to his fingertips. 'Tara can do a bit of spadework, though, while you and I have that talk we've promised ourselves.'

Once more, Kemp met Sally's eyes. She gave him the smallest nod in return, telling him she could handle it.

'Just one thing, then, before I go,' he told Mark, hard-eyed. 'This is Sally's deal. Understood?'

The other man nodded. 'Understood.'

Kemp studied him for a moment, then sprang to his

feet with an air of distasteful duty done. 'That lets us out, then, Tara. Will you be kind enough to have coffee with me at the house?'

'Love to, darling!' Tara rose with a radiant, meaningful smile for Sally. 'See you in the taxi to the airport, poppets.'

'They're a couple already.' Mark watched the two departing figures, one all sober strength and the other all floating grace. 'See?' as they paused in the archway, and Kemp offered his arm. 'He can't keep his hands off her.'

Trust him to put it like that! Sally welcomed the arrival of the coffee, and poured her own at once. It was too hot to drink, but she could at least keep it here under her nose, its wholesome aroma crowding out the spicy aftershave which had suddenly begun to oppress her.

'So here we are.' Mark had taken a cigarillo from the pack which had arrived with the coffee, and now had his monogrammed gold lighter poised. 'Partners in spite of ourselves.'

For how long? Sally wondered as he lit up. 'Please feel free to smoke,' she said drily.

'I do, I do.' The tiny dark wand glowed between his lips, faded between his fingers. 'And don't worry, the account's yours.'

'So Kemp said.'

He bridled. 'Whittaker doesn't control my private life!'

'I doubt if he'd want to.'

'No?' Mark smirked. 'Well, he's just accepted my free gift of a nice little piece of it. If you hadn't guessed.'

'I didn't have to *guess*.'

'She told you, did she?' He seemed gratified. 'It's all in the past now. Off with the old, on with the new.'

Sally had taken up her coffee, but now put it down untasted. 'What new?'

'The very newest.' He tapped off the first tiny cylinder of ash. 'The totally untried, in fact.'

The green eyes fixed hers in one of those hypnotic stares. Sally returned it, stiffening her resolve, and it was he who finally broke away to raise the cigarillo once more to his lips.

Couldn't he *see* how she felt about him? Or did he just not care? Sally looked at her cooling coffee and wished her stomach hadn't closed up on her. The sooner she could drink this, the sooner she could get out of here.

She heard Mark speak as if from a distance, and came to herself with a start. 'The what?'

'The Mile High Club.' He settled smugly to the job of explaining. 'You've heard of it?'

'I've heard silly jokes about sex in aeroplanes.'

'They're not jokes. If you haven't made it in a plane, you haven't lived. Now,' he leant forward, blowing smoke into her face, 'I'm planning a whole new category.'

Sally nodded, dumb. Maybe he wouldn't suggest what she feared he was going to.

But he did. 'You and I are going to found the Mile High First Time Ever Club. On our flight home.'

She'd heard, but she still couldn't believe it. She sat transfixed, not able to convince herself that this was really happening to her.

'Here's what we do. . .' Mark was going on.

Yes, he'd worked out every sordid detail of how it could be managed without attracting too much attention.

'We don't want the stewardess hassling us,' he finished, and drew on his cigarillo, alight with his vision.

'And th-this is what I have to do, to keep the account?' Sally queried.

'Of course not!' His surprise was quite genuine. 'You do it for fun. It's the chance of a lifetime for you.'

She sat very still, trying to think through the roaring dark that surrounded her. Everything seemed to have gone a long way off. Even her head had gone a long way from the rest of her.

'I'm glad old Barnes is booked on that flight,' mused Mark. 'There's Tara, of course, but men make more convincing witnesses.'

'W-witnesses?'

Her lips could hardly form the word. Once it was out, though, the enormity of it gave her strength, and she found she was on her feet. The scrape of her chair echoed in her ears as she stared down at the narrow, unruffled blond head. How clean it looked—far too clean for what went on inside it.

'You don't want your coffee?' Mark glanced at her full cup. 'I wouldn't have ordered it if I'd known——'

'I agree it would be a pity to waste it.'

Rage sang in her ears, armoured her, set her apart as she picked up the gold-edged cup. She carried it, rock-steady, to his side of the table, and carefully poured its contents over his head.

CHAPTER EIGHT

THE odd thing was how soon it was over. Already it had become a memory, the creamy-brown coffee turning to sludge as it darkened Mark's hair and dripped to his eyebrows. Sally's feet must have rushed her to the exit, because her next view was of a waiter hurrying by with twitching lips and poised napkin. The last was from a distance, of Mark dabbing his face while the waiter mopped at the mud-coloured stains on the light suit.

In the lobby, she made a detour to the reception desk.

'Er—I seem to have this cup.'

She set it down with a glassy smile, and made off before the clerk could ask questions. Then she was out under the chestnut trees, gulping clean air.

'So that's that. No Kingfisher account.' She set her tired feet to the hill. 'No typing even, if Mark has any influence!'

And it didn't matter. Soothed by sun-polished meadows and snow-cooled breezes, her muscles stopped complaining and settled to the climb. She felt as if they were lifting her right out of the grubby world she had accepted so blindly until five days ago.

I'll go home, she decided. Maybe Dr Aitken still wants a secretary. If he doesn't, somebody will.

It wasn't the most exciting prospect, but so much the better. She'd had more than enough excitement—certainly of the kind you got at Limelight.

145

How could I have stuck it so long? she marvelled. It's all stoats and rabbits there—eat or be eaten!

Above her in the meadow she could see the Herdis, man and wife, cutting hay on land too steep for a tractor. They worked intently, and the scent rolled down the slope like balm. Sally felt it soaking into her, slowing her down, strengthening and clearing her mind for her final task in this beautiful place which had so changed her outlook on life.

Hadn't it? Something had, and it wasn't loathsome Mark. She knew now that she had met lots like him during her time at Limelight.

He's only an extreme version, she thought, marvelling that she hadn't seen it before. More conspicuous because he's trying so hard, on that pile of stuff Kemp wouldn't name before a lady.

She halted on the smooth little ribbon of asphalt, washed by laughter that was near to tears. She could see it so clear, the barnyard where Mark flapped his wings and crowed while stupid hens like Tara, as she had been herself, scratched and strutted and crooned their admiration.

She knew now what had changed her, and it wasn't stoat-rooster Mark. Even this high country of snowy peaks and precious, toiled-over earth had only played a background part.

It's Kemp who's shown me what a real man should be, she admitted as she set off again. And to think I called him old-fashioned, because he reckons women are ladies!

As if it was old-fashioned to consider others, and honour your obligations, and protect instead of exploiting.

Which would you rather be, she asked herself on the

farmhouse steps, one of Kemp's ladies, or one of Mark's hens?

Not that she had any more choice to be either. At the door, fatigue smothered her like a blanket when she sought for her key and realised it was still in her tracksuit pocket. That meant she'd have to find it in her suitcase, once she'd entered here without being seen by. . .by the two already within.

The casement window of the corridor stood wide to the May sunshine. In silence Sally braced her arms and sprang to sit on the sill, folded her legs through, and dropped to the other side.

As soon as she was in she could hear them, down at the far end of the living-room where they couldn't be seen through the open doorway. Good, so they wouldn't see her either, and she could be upstairs before they were any the wiser. As she crept to the foot of the stairs the voices came again, the feminine and the deeply, warmly masculine, both making wordless noises. . .

Sally grabbed the stair-rail. It wasn't. It couldn't be! She couldn't be standing here listening to Tara's gasps and rhythmic little moans, Kemp's muffled, answering murmurs.

A sharp pain in her fingers brought her to herself— her nails had been trying to dig holes in the banister. She stole up the stairs and sat shakily on the alpine chair which Kemp had put back in its place by the window.

I never really believed it till now, she realised. I never believed he'd buy Tara's act at all, let alone. . .

Let alone make love to her in that special, beautiful room below. This house, Sally realised, and above all its living-room, had settled in her mind as a place of cleanliness and peace, a pavilion of light between mountains and valley, a memory she had believed couldn't be taken away from her.

And now it's gone, she thought. She unpacked her tracksuit, pincered the key from its pocket between reluctant finger and thumb, and dropped it on the tall chest of drawers in front of the tiny mirror. Even Mark, last night, couldn't destroy it the way they just have.

She could never come back here, not even in her mind. Trying to come to terms with the idea, she turned from her own burning-eyed image to try and re-pack her case. Only the damned thing was all messed up now, wasn't it? And she had to start over.

'And I don't need this, anyway.' She rolled the hateful red dress into a ball and hurled it to the bed. 'Let *him* be the one to get rid of it, and remember why it's torn!'

Not that it would mean a thing to him now. Sally toiled to reorganise the suitcase, and presently it closed. As she checked the room one last time, the voices floated up from the hall.

'. . .still not too urgent.' That was Kemp. 'It's only an hour to the airport.'

'Fine.' That was Tara's coo, still slightly roughened. 'I'm glad I'll have time to. . .freshen up. . .'

I bet you are, Sally thought savagely. Only 'freshen' isn't the word I'd have used!

She couldn't really be inhaling Tara's expensive rose and cedar perfume, not up the stairs and through the closed door. But if she were, then out with it. She dared a little snort through her nostrils as the front door opened and closed.

In a minute she'd be able to make all the noise she wanted. She could shout and scream, curse Tara's cardboard prettiness and shoddy pretences, swear loud hatred of Kemp who had been taken in by them. Most of all she could vent her scorn for herself, for ever having been taken in by *him*.

'Man of truth, indeed!' she rasped as their voices came to her again through the open window. 'You're as bad as she is. Or if you're not, you soon will be— she'll see to that.'

'Don't worry, I'll make sure she doesn't.' He might have been answering from below. 'She knows the time of the plane—she must be on her way here by now, to fetch her things.'

'He's talking about me.' Sally ducked to the window.

She couldn't see their faces, but she didn't need to. They'd stopped talking and were crossing the road, close-linked, shaggy dark head stooped to fluffy fair, wool-clad arm round silken shoulders. When they reached his car, Kemp settled Tara in it like jewellery in a case.

'I suppose she's much too precious to walk down the hill like the rest of us,' Sally taunted the closed-up car.

Her own voice, so thin on the empty air, sent her hurrying to the wardrobe. Before the car's purr had died away she was down the stairs, lightweight jacket over one arm, bag slung from her shoulder, case dragging from one hand.

She couldn't risk saying goodbye to the house. She mustn't catch the fragrance of basil from the kitchen, or of beeswax and turpentine from the carved furniture, or of the heady white lilac she'd arranged yesterday in the silver vase Kemp had won on some long-ago school sports day.

Would she ever be able to forget his shy grin as he'd handed over that vase? Maybe, a hundred years from now. But not if she smelt that lilac, and especially not if it were overlaid, like the air out here in the hall, with the scent of rose and cedar.

Even outside the door it wasn't easy, assaulted once more by the scent of new-mown hay. If she lived at home, as she meant to, she would have to endure something like this all through the summer. Whenever her father mowed his fields, she'd have to remember. . .

I won't. She took the steps at a laboured run, dragged down by the case. He isn't worth it. And he isn't worth crying about either.

She sniffed violently, blinked her hardest, and set off down the hill without a backward glance. Let her smarting eyes dare to overflow, just let them dare! Well, one tear, then. Not enough to mop, not enough to halt for when you had a plane to catch, and the taxi would soon be arriving. . .

The taxi!

She dropped the suitcase in the middle of the road and sat on it, regardless of its bulging edges. Until now, she'd thought of her journey home only in terms of the plane. She could stay away from Mark before take-off and after landing, and he always travelled first class, so she'd known she needn't suffer him on board. But why, why, why had she forgotten until now that the village had only one taxi?

I should have caught the bus, she fumed, and then the train from the valley.

But it was too late for any of that. The only way she would make the flight she had booked was to travel to the airport in a small, enclosed space, with or without Tara, but certainly with poisonous Mark Walsh whom she had publicly humiliated.

'I'll just have to miss my booking again,' she announced to the deep blue empty sky. 'I'll get there when I can, and take whatever plane's going.'

So she had plenty of time to sit here, and imagine

how it would be to wait all night for a plane. To linger like a ghost in the roaring bustle and flat, everlasting light of international traffic, as different from this quiet sunshine as Mark Walsh was different from Kemp Whittaker.

I never really believed it would happen, she realised miserably. Deep down, I hoped I'd stay here forever.

Why, the first thing to pop into her mind, while she had been up-ending that coffee-cup, had been how Kemp would like hearing about this.

What an idiot!

She tried to laugh at herself, but the laugh ended in a sob, and the sob in a full-throated keening. The tears burst through at last, and the ex-efficient, ex-successful Sally Benedict sat on her suitcase in the middle of the empty road from Engeldorf to the forest, crying like a mountain torrent. Like two mountain torrents. Noisy ones.

'Not another weeping woman!'

Sally stopped in mid-sniffle. Yes, it was Kemp all right, just getting out of his car parked lower on the road. He must have glided up when she was otherwise occupied.

She blew resoundingly into her fifth tissue. 'Can't a person have a private cry?'

'On a public highway?' He was at her side, knees doubled comfortably to her level. 'When she's set the whole village by the ears?'

'What?' She sat up, and tucked the tissue away with the other four. 'How have I done that?'

'You mean you don't *remember* publicly assaulting one of the hotel's most valuable guests?'

'I only——'

'I heard.' Kemp sounded regretful. 'Wish I'd been there.'

'Yes, well, you can't be everywhere.' The pain twisted, and she rushed on, 'Are they all very angry with me?'

'The staff are acting as if you did them a favour. Though I don't know,' he acknowledged, 'about the manager.'

'I must have lost him all the Kingfisher business.'

'Not as long as Walsh sees a profit in it. You've certainly made sure he'll never pay another personal visit, though,' Kemp added with satisfaction. 'And that's great news.'

'So you'll be left here in peace.'

She couldn't keep the longing out of her voice. It would be Tara enjoying the peace, and she wouldn't appreciate it at all. . .

'Tara doesn't appreciate it at all.'

This was the second time he'd answered her thought—had he got inside her head or something? She turned sideways to stare into the deep-set, diamond-clear eyes.

'Walsh took the taxi off early,' he explained. 'I think he has some idea they'll do a better clean-up on him at the airport.' He consulted his watch. 'Don't worry, we've got time.'

'You mean you're going to drive me?'

'That's what I came out to tell you. This way,' he hastily covered his own kindness, 'maybe I'll get to see the stains before they're cleaned off. That's better,' as he noted her watery smile. 'They say the tie's gone from sickly green to khaki.'

'He's not having much luck with his ties. . .'

Sally hiccuped to silence. Here they were, joking about it exactly as she'd subconsciously imagined, in spite of Kemp's being committed to another woman.

Another woman who would see that she kept her hold on him.

'What was that about Tara?' she asked, determined to get the worst over. 'So she's in the same fix?'

'I should think she's better off this way,' he answered shortly. 'But yes, she's meeting us in the lobby with her gear.' He offered his hands, and when Sally refused them, took possession of hers and drew her to her feet. 'Why were *you* crying?'

She looked away from him, pulling her hands out of that big, warm grasp. 'None of your business.'

'Was it something Walsh said to you? There's still time for me to knock his teeth down his throat.'

'I don't know how you've the nerve, Kemp Whittaker!' She stalked past him to the car. 'You'd better save that stuff for. . .for where it belongs!'

'What stuff?' He opened the door for her.

'I think you know.'

She flopped into the seat, and pulled the door shut on his enquiring face. Only when she saw him stowing her suitcase did she remember she'd left it in the road. Feeling foolish, she said nothing more for the two minutes it took to reach the village, and, as soon as he had parked under the chestnut trees, hurried with him into the hotel.

Tara's travel organiser was gold-brown kid, and her sand-grey suit set off her fairness to perfection. How many outfits had the woman packed for one night, anyway, in that gold-brown suitcase?

'Three outfits, for one night,' murmured Kemp, uncannily among her thoughts again. 'I wonder how she looks in jeans?'

'Stunning, no doubt,' Sally snapped.

What else could she say? That she'd never seen her junior in trousers of any kind, not even for a barbecue?

And that she strongly suspected that Tara's skirts, always pleated or floating or loosely gathered, disguised over-large hips and short legs? It would only sound bitchy.

And Tara certainly looked stunning now, though perhaps not as radiant as you might expect. A closer view showed her eyes rather heavy, and her lips a little swollen.

From kissing, Sally thought, hating them both.

'Recovered?' Kemp had greeted Tara with a pat on the cheek. 'Yes, I can see you have. Now, shall I put this case in the car?'

'Thanks, darling.'

The stuck-on lashes fluttered—surely they were carrying more mascara than usual? They were so weighed down, it was a wonder they didn't fall off. They *were* falling off—one had already detached itself at the outer corner.

'Oh, dear!' Tara hid the threatened eye under a lacy hanky, and turned away. 'It's no use, darling, I'm afraid I'll have to go back to my room.'

'Plenty of time.'

Kemp's voice was low and soothing, but his hand closed on Sally's wrist. Indignant, bewildered, she felt herself dragged after Tara who, face still half hidden, was in the lift by the time they reached it.

She's pretending to *cry*! Sally fumed to herself. But no, she thought as a tear left a white, mascara-bordered track through the paint, she wouldn't let that happen on purpose. She *is* crying.

'Off you go,' Kemp ordered. 'Do what you can for her.'

'Me?' Sally gaped at him.

'I thought I'd got her through it, but I hadn't.' He

pushed Sally into the lift. 'Maybe another woman can help more.'

Mystified, Sally allowed the lift doors to close with herself inside. As soon as they did Tara scrabbled in her travel organiser, black-edged tears running unchecked, both sets of lashes drooping ever further like centipede eye-patches. How could you not feel sorry for her? Sally found a tissue in her own bag, and deftly picked off each set of soaked lashes in turn to fold in soft paper and offer back.

'Th-thanks.' Tara, oddly bird-like now her round little eyes had lost their sooty fringes, rejected the offer. 'I've s-some s-spares. . . Oh, s-sardines,' on a fresh storm of tears, 'why is everything so g-gruesome!'

The schoolgirl slang was forlornly touching. Sally gently lifted away the wide-open, chaotic organiser bag, put an arm round her junior, and, when they reached the second floor, supported her like a lost little girl to her room.

A cleaning-woman was already hanging the duvets out on the balcony. Returning through the window, she stared in alarm, which quickly turned to sympathy, as Tara flung herself on one of the still-sheeted beds and gave way to her misery.

'She'll be all right.' Sally pointed to her watch and held up her ten spread fingers. 'Ten minutes? Please?'

The woman offered tea and, when it was refused, departed with the duvet covers.

'There, there.' Sally sat on the bed and patted the heaving shoulders, feeling ineffectual.

'L-last night after the p-party,' Tara's voice came out muffled by the pillow, 'he c-called me a s-slut!'

Sally felt her mouth tighten with the now-familiar distaste. So Mark's reaction to her own refusal had been to take it out on another woman. But why had the other woman been available? Hadn't she been at the castle after all?

'And then he made love. . .'

'He did *what*?'

'Do grow up, Sally!'

The little bird-face, exotically striped blue and black and pink, turned on the make-up-stained pillow. The superior tone would have been funny if it hadn't been so sad.

'That was the deal for the trip. Only,' the words slurred, 'I didn't expect him to do it as if he hated me!'

The sobs were muffled once more in the pillow. Sally patted rhythmically, like a mother quieting a baby, and stared at the other bed. The two formed a double in the local style, together but made up separately, and yes, the pillow and sheet had been used. And now Tara was paying the price in self-disgust.

It was hard to know what to say. Pointing out that she wasn't acting grown-up at the moment would only have added to her misery. Telling her she'd been silly wouldn't help either—she must know it. No, all you could do was sympathise, in wordless murmurs, through the gasps and rhythmic little moans. . .

Another weeping woman.

'Did you tell Kemp about this?' Sally asked.

'Of course not!' Tara raised her head, diverted at last by what she clearly considered another silly question. 'You *never* tell your present man about the last.'

'Only he isn't your present man, is he? All he offered you,' Sally went on in joyous conviction, 'was a shoulder to cry on.'

'He s-said. . .' a new storm of sobs threatened '. . .he s-said I was t-too p-popular.'

'And that upset you?' Sally was puzzled, until she remembered Kemp's instinctive courtesy towards women. 'Popular' was probably the best word he could think of, not to be too hurtful. 'So he turned you down,' she concluded, 'and you cried.'

'He didn't really turn me down,' Tara asserted, pride returning. 'I mean, he wasn't rude or anything. Not like Mark. . .that was it, really,' she added, unravelling the reasons for her present weakness. 'If people are nasty you can fight them, but if they're nice. . .' She dabbed back the new tears which threatened, and distracted herself by sitting up, round eyes inquisitive. 'What on earth did you do to Mark last night to put him in such a mood?'

'Locked him out. Just as you should have done,' Sally added.

'Yes, well, I didn't expect to be here at all, did I?' The tears gathered. 'I asked and asked Kemp about the inside of the castle. . .'

'And still he brought you back to the hotel?'

'He didn't even do that.' An angry sniffle. 'He got me a lift from the hotel manager. He's nice, isn't he?' The blue eyes regained some of their shrewdness. 'I could work with him.'

'He's getting married next week,' Sally said drily, 'to a girl from Klosters. I expect he went to the party for an hour, just to——'

'I'm talking *business*,' Tara interrupted with dignity. '*He* doesn't like Mark either; I could tell when he was apologising about the taxi.' She almost smiled, reviving at last. 'I wish it had been me who poured coffee over Mark.'

'It's not exactly the way to get on in business.'

'No,' Tara agreed, nearly herself again. 'And in business I can really reach him.' She stood up, claimed her organiser bag, and made for the bathroom. 'I know all the Kingfisher clients. . . Sardines, look at me!' Her streaked, accusing face reappeared round the door. 'Is this how I was downstairs, in public?'

'Nothing like,' Sally assured her. 'What was that about Kingfisher clients?'

'I don't suppose *they* like Mark any more than the rest of us,' Tara trilled over the rattle of pots and potions being set ready below the glass. 'I bet they'd prefer travelling with a firm called. . .' pause for thought '. . .called *Queen*fisher.'

'You wouldn't!' Sally hurried into the bathroom, shocked.

'Offer a better deal? Why not?' Hair tucked into a plastic cap, eyes shut, Tara was happily creaming her face. 'Queenfisher would work direct with the hotels, and do its own publicity.'

'But. . .you can't just set up a business like that. . .'

'Watch me.' The cold cream yielded to a series of tissues. 'I can get at least three backers, just for the asking.' The little bird-face emerged, naked and shiny, yet attractive with this new light in the blue eyes. 'I've been wondering ever since I left college where I'm going, and now I know.'

'What about finding the right sort of guy?'

'The right sort of guy,' Tara turned on the tap, 'is one who'll help me see off Mark Walsh.'

'Tara, do be careful! You're taking on a bad enemy.'

'I know what I'm doing.' Tara splashed and lathered. 'You wait! I'll smash Kingfisher to little——' She broke off as a firm knock sounded at the outer door. 'If that's Kemp, don't let him in. I won't be seen till I've got myself in order.'

'A whole paint job?' Sally glanced at her watch as the knock sounded again. 'Won't that take hours?'

'It takes a while, but I've got time.' Tara rinsed, and

lovingly patted her face dry. 'I'm not going on that plane after all.'

'You're not?' Sally floundered for her bearings. 'So we're to go without you?'

'That's right.' A smug smile lengthened the pale, too-thin lips. 'Enjoy your flight, darling.'

'What about the campaign to smash Kingfisher?'

'That starts right here, with the manager of this hotel.'

'Anybody home?' It was Kemp, cautiously opening the door.

'Not yet, darling, but I will be.' The smile spread to the thin-lashed, bead-blue eyes. 'I will be.'

'You can't mean to try again. . .on. . .' Sally couldn't say it, not with Kemp near enough to hear them. 'After. . .'

'Maybe all I need is time. And it's certainly worth trying for. That,' Tara murmured very low to the reflection which her reflected hands were covering with flesh-tinted foundation, 'is a real man. Off you go, darling,' she added briskly. 'I want to lock the door.'

'What do you mean, you're not ready but you will be?' Kemp had closed the outer door. 'It's now or not at all.'

Sally came out into the room. 'She's decided she's staying.'

The bathroom lock clicked, and Tara's voice carolled from within. 'Don't worry about me, darlings. Go ahead without me.'

'At least she's cheered up.' Kemp crossed the room, and met Sally at the foot of the bed. 'What's this latest maggot?'

'Maggot?' She stared up at him in bewilderment.

'Malarkey.' He nodded towards the locked bathroom. 'Bushwa. Flim-flam.' He shook his shaggy mane,

angry with himself for not putting it more clearly.
'What's she up to now?'

Sally tried to drag her gaze off him, and couldn't.
She must use every minute left to her, memorise every
line, every movement, every passing mood of those
tough, gentle, passionate features. The impatience that
curled his lip at the moment was for Tara, and so was
the sardonic tilt of his brows, but both were precious,
living images to hoard for the empty years to come.

'I'll. . .explain. . .presently,' she managed at last.

'The hell with it!' He loomed nearer. 'We've better
things to talk about, you and I.'

'There isn't much time——'

'We'll make time.' He drew her into the scent of
pine and fern and musk, and that dear, dear mouth
took hers.

It felt so right. So good. She'd been waiting all her
life to be stirred like this, tormented like this, filled
with this strange fullness which led only to a deeper
need. His hand cupped the back of her head, his fingers
stroked her nape, played down her spine, and at last
pressed her, natural as sunshine, to that male desire
which seemed already part of herself.

'It. . .it must be something about these hotel rooms,'
she murmured at last against the roughness of his
cheek.

'It's something about you.' Kemp blew a strand of
hair away from her forehead. 'My beautiful brown wild
creature. . .' His lips closed her eyes, and his tongue
flicked her lashes. 'These are real, aren't they?'

'Such as they are.'

'They're gorgeous, and so are you.' He tilted her
chin, placing her so that he could once more claim her
mouth.

Sally held back. 'We shouldn't be doing this. . .'

As if to prove her point, a no-nonsense tap at the door gave them just time to spring apart. The cleaning-woman, prompt to the agreed ten minutes, addressed Kemp austerely in her own language. He replied briefly, then rapped the bathroom door.

'Tara!' The tone might have been a father to a tiresome child. 'Do I gather you're staying on here?'

'Still there, darlings?' The coo pierced the door like a gimlet. 'You'll miss the plane if you don't hurry.'

'That's our problem. Yours is to come out here and give the staff some idea what to expect.'

'All in good time, darling.'

'It needs settling now.' Kemp's brows had drawn together. 'The cleaning-lady's asking what to do about the room.'

'Oh. I did think I'd keep it, but. . .' the coo faltered '. . . I'll ask for another instead. I don't like this one.'

'So ask for it, and let her finish refitting here.'

'Why? Does somebody else want it?'

'I don't know.' Kemp threw a glance at the woman who waited, severe in her white overall, to be allowed to get on with her job. 'But cleaning-staff have a schedule to meet, like anybody else.'

'Is that all? Tell her I'll be ready in half an hour.'

'Half an hour!' Kemp bellowed. 'Hell's bells, woman, are you painting the Sydney Harbour Bridge? How long does it take to glue a new set of——?'

He stopped there because Sally had hurriedly put her hand over his mouth. He grabbed it away, drew breath to shout again, and instead let out a great, releasing sigh. Then, finding he still had her hand close to his face, he kissed the palm.

Which made it difficult, but not impossible, to break away and confront the ever sterner cleaning-woman. Sally was about to try explaining in English when Kemp rattled something over her shoulder. The woman responded with a disapproval that bristled from every line of her sturdy figure, and made a dignified exit.

'It's silly to get on the wrong side of the staff,' Sally murmured as Kemp rejoined her, 'if you want to do business here.'

'Who wants to do business here?' He put an arm round her, urging her gently to the door.

'Tara does. She——'

'Forget Tara.' He bundled her along the corridor and into the lift. 'You've got a plane to catch, not to mention hearing my proposition.'

'What p-proposition?'

'Strictly honourable, I promise. And to prove it——' he raised both hands in the air like a man at gunpoint, and stood back to the far wall of the descending lift '—I won't touch you again.'

'You won't?' Sally asked, downcast. 'Wh-why not?'

'We'll talk on the way to the airport.'

So he meant to be rid of her. When the lift brought them to the ground floor, she hurried with him to the car in depressed silence. Whatever made him think she didn't want him to touch her? And a proposition, however honourable, wasn't a proposal.

And that's what I want, she realised as they glided through the village. I always have. I feel as if I've wanted to marry Kemp Whittaker all my life.

The road to the valley, well engineered but steeply twisting, claimed all his attention. She understood why he wouldn't yet put his proposition, whatever it was, but the waiting was hard. Every downward curve took her further from the farmhouse and castle, further from Kemp's enchanting, enchanted world of mountain and forest which might have been hers if only. . . And he was never even going to touch her again.

'Right.' He waited to turn into the straight road along the floor of the valley. 'It isn't much, I know. We're so quiet here, and this is where I like to be.' He edged out behind a minibus full of children. 'And I don't know what your Limelight salary is, but I doubt if I can match it——'

'Are you offering me a job?' she interrupted, scarcely daring to hope. 'Here? And, if so, why are we rushing for this plane?'

He shot her a glance. 'You don't want to know the terms?'

'Kemp, I love Engeldorf. It's like being told I can live in heaven. I'd. . .' She sought a way of showing how serious she was. 'I'd wash dishes. Scrub floors. . .'

'Sort specimens? Keep records? Tidy all that stuff I've got in the castle?'

'I thought. . .outsiders. . .weren't welcome there.' Seeing his enquiring frown, Sally hastened to explain. 'You wouldn't let Tara——'

'That little pest! I suppose Jacqui Lane had her uses after all,' Kemp added as if his old love were some tiresome insect. 'She did teach me to see through phoneys like herself.'

'So I'm to work in the castle.' Sally smiled at the angelic little boy in the back of the minibus, then noticed a motorway sign. 'Let's turn round now.'

His only answer was to set the car towards Zurich and its airport. 'You'll need to work your notice, pack, sort things out. Above all, you've got to think this over.' He overtook the minibus. 'Get a clear idea of the risks you'd be running.'

'What risks?' Sally asked, newly tense.

'I'm not about to ask you to marry me. . .'

'I wouldn't dream of accepting if you did,' she lied, stung. 'I've only known you six days.'

'Exactly. On the other hand, I do very badly want to make love to you—in case you hadn't noticed.' Kemp flashed her a sideways glance. 'And the flesh is weak. I can try not to, but I can't guarantee it.'

'Maybe I wouldn't mind too much if you did.' Which must be the understatement of the year!

'You'd mind. Whatever you think now, you'd mind like hell.' He eased up to the maximum permitted speed. 'For you, it's total commitment or nothing.'

Sally nodded, faced with the facts of her own character. 'And you,' she swallowed her humiliation, forced herself to accept it, 'don't feel you can offer that.'

'After six days,' Kemp returned doggedly, 'neither of us can.'

'It's not like you to be so cautious.'

'Would you rather I pretended——?'

'No!' It was out before she knew it. 'You couldn't.'

'What makes you so sure?' he demanded, still with his argument. 'What have you learnt about me, in six days?'

'I've learnt that much. If you pretended anything, anything at all, you wouldn't be. . .'

She trailed off, unable to finish in the only way she wanted. If Kemp didn't value truth more than easy promises, more than pleasure, far above the games of profit and loss which were all she'd understood until she met him, he wouldn't be the man she loved. And she mustn't say that, because he wasn't offering love in return. All she could do was accept what he could truthfully give—a new start, friendship, employment, and the risk of breaking her heart.

She stared in silence at the ever-changing views. Slopes ran up to cliffs which opened to new, herd-dotted slopes. Farms and villages and small towns

glowed in the reddening sun, bright with the care of
countless hard-working generations.

'That's the Walensee,' Kemp told her presently as a
blue lake spread to their left with more mountains
beyond.

'And it's only one of dozens!' she breathed,
enchanted. 'It's no contest, really.'

'What isn't?' He switched on the headlights for a
tunnel.

'Whether I come back here,' Sally sighed as they
glided into the sunshine on the other side of another
mountain. 'I suppose I do have to catch this old plane?'

'Unless you intend——' he eyed her casual outfit
'——to settle here with nothing but two pairs of jeans
and three T-shirts.'

'Which reminds me. . .' she shifted, and stretched
'. . .didn't you say you were putting Tara's case in the
back?'

'Hell!' He slapped a hand to his forehead. 'I'll have
to give it in at the hotel.' He shot Sally a piteous
glance. 'Do you think I'll be able to dodge her?'

'I doubt it,' Sally giggled. 'You'd better hole up in
the castle with the door locked, till I get back.'

He joined in her laughter. 'Protecting me from
women like that's going to be one of your duties.'

'Sir.' She sketched a salute. 'Shall I tell you another?'

'Hang on, who's the employer round here?'

'You are, and you're going to live up to it,' she told
him severely. 'Nothing in the world would ever make
you elegant. . .'

'Heaven forbid!'

'. . .but at least I can see you have regular haircuts.'

'Dammit, Sally——'

'No haircuts, no deal.'

'All right,' Kemp conceded with mock reluctance.
'But you're a hard woman, Sally Benedict.'

CHAPTER NINE

AT TIMES, Sally felt like Delilah with a shorn Samson.

Though Kemp's as strong as ever, she argued to herself. And his hair's not much changed.

The stylist he called a barber had only taken off a little and skilfully shaped the rest. Now it was meant to cling round his ears and wave close to the grand outlines of his head—and so it would, if he'd stop messing it up while he worked. But he wouldn't, and he'd never remember to tidy it either. Just look at him there through the window, leaving the castle by its massive outer door to take the forest track to the village.

She opened the casement. 'Have you a comb?'

'Is it that bad?' Kemp frowned up from the courtyard.

'Nothing I can't fix, if you'll come over here.'

He hesitated, then reluctantly crossed the cobbles and stood under the window. From her higher inside level, she leant across the deep stone sill and pushed his still-damp hair to the lines it was supposed to follow. The dear, springy tufts rebelled and rioted through her fingers, but their owner simply waited, granite-faced, until she had patted them to some sort of order.

'Satisfied?' he asked at last.

And how could she say she wasn't? How remind him of a time he wouldn't have let her hands go without kissing them? All she could do was nod, tight-lipped as

166

himself, and assure him again that no, she didn't want
to walk with him to the post office.

'I'll stay here and get our *raclette*.'

'There's no need for that,' he told her with one of
those thin, forced smiles he was always giving her
nowadays.

'I want to.' She fanned the July heat from her long-
sleeved, high-necked, unseasonably heavy blouse.
'And then I'll shower.'

'I don't know why you swathed yourself like that. I
said the wasps wouldn't sting us.'

'I'd almost rather they had. Then I'd have *known*
how it felt, instead of just imagining it.'

He nodded briefly, raised a hand in farewell, and
loped off through the stone archway.

In the old days, he'd have called me chicken or
something, she reflected, left alone in the once terrifying giant's den. And I'd have told him to stop bullying,
and we'd have had one of those lovely rows. . .

She sighed, and turned back to the study-bedroom
which had become their improvised workplace. The
cameras, tape-recorder and specimens were safe in
their cupboards, and she'd washed the dregs of coffee
from the thermos. So at last she could take her towel,
and the fresh clothes she had brought up from her own
lodging in the farmhouse, and head for his shower.

'If only he weren't so damned *polite*!' Hair dried to
a silky cloud, Sally buttoned herself into the new, fern-
patterned dress. 'If he gets near me by accident, he
apologises. But mostly he doesn't get near me.'

'Oh, well.' She wandered across the corridor to enjoy
the newly finished drawing-room. 'It's a great life, for
all that.'

She turned this way and that in the empty, many-
windowed room, enchanted as ever by its magnificent

proportions. What chandeliers they'd find for this newly restored ceiling, what carpets for the newly sealed parquet, what couches and chairs to set off the newly-gilded curves of the white baroque stove! This part of the castle had been added in the elegant eighteenth century, so the furniture must fit.

Searching for it would be a long, delightful task. She'd been thrilled when Kemp had asked for her help on it, but he'd only shrugged.

'I said you'd be doing a bit of everything, didn't I?'

He had, and she did. In her month here she had filed his letters, answered them, and logged his phone calls. She had labelled the display cabinets he'd had built in the long, empty-shelved room he called the library, and then she'd arranged in them all the carefully-sorted collections of fossils and photos, butterflies and bones which had lain about the castle in every corner that wasn't being refurbished.

Last week she'd driven round the local farms for supplies. Yesterday she had typed his notes on the object, earthy one side and honeycombed with paper cells the other, which he said was part of an old wasp-nest. Today they had spent looking for this year's nest, and tomorrow she was to go with him to Zurich and offer her views on furniture.

'It's a marvellous job.' Sally set to work in the austere bachelor kitchen which had served Kemp up here so far. 'And I love it just as much as I thought I would. So what's gone wrong?'

Whatever it was, it had already begun when she had first seen Kemp in London. He had spent two weeks there, living in his Baker Street flat and putting the finishing touches to his latest series while she worked out her notice at Limelight.

When he had first called at her office to take her to

dinner, she'd hardly recognised him. It wasn't just the new-style hair, or the dark suit and white shirt and impeccably polished shoes.

Even toned down like that, he's too big for city life, she mused. Only—where did the wildness go?

Why did he speak in such muted tones, disagree so quietly, accept so patiently the endless requests for autographs? Above all, why did he stay so very distant?

'I know you promised not to touch me,' Sally had argued the first time he had helped her out of her jacket at arm's length. 'But you needn't treat me as if I had the plague!'

'I'll do it my way, if you don't mind.'

And he had gone on staying in the far corner of taxis, and refusing to visit her flat even to pick her up for the evening.

Only her family's invitation to spend a weekend with them had brought out the old warmth. She had passed it on shyly, hoping that Kemp wouldn't guess her parents' resolve to vet this well-known personality who was to be their daughter's new employer. If he wouldn't go to Newton, they were quite capable of turning up in Engeldorf. In fact, they probably would anyway, she had realised with a shudder.

But if Kemp understood any of that, he didn't mind. 'Why, that's marvellous!' he'd exclaimed. 'I'd love to.'

'Don't expect anything. . . I mean, it's very quiet. . .'

'And you think that'll worry me? Don't you know me at all yet, Sally?'

And maybe she didn't. In Newton he had opened out completely, helped her father on the farm, eaten hugely of her mother's cooking, and gone out with her brother to the compost heap where Simon had found what he thought might be the eggs of a slow-worm.

The pair of them had returned at teatime with excited accounts of baby slow-worms hatching under their very eyes.

'I wish I'd had my camera,' Simon said, 'but it's something to have seen it.'

'I wish you weren't going so far away,' Sally's father said, appearing in her room to carry down her suitcase. 'But it's something to have seen him.'

'You like him,' Sally stated, not needing to ask.

In the kitchen, her mother packed the usual roast chicken, new-laid eggs, home-grown lettuce and tomatoes, and Sally's favourite gingerbread. When Sally appeared, she was just adding the rest of the marble cake Kemp had enjoyed.

'That, Sarah Benedict, is a young man in a million,' she told her daughter.

'Not that young,' Sally objected. 'He's thirty-two.'

'A nice age,' her mother retorted with sinister promptness.

Well, at least they hadn't quizzed Kemp about his income, and his past, and his plans for the future. Though he'd given away something of those without being asked.

'I'm having at least a year off show business,' he'd told them. 'I want to write about the birds and animals and plants round Engeldorf.'

And that was what he was doing now. Already the book was organised into sections, and, with the two of them on it, material was piling up. He said she saved him hours of work.

'And so I do,' she agreed.

She again admired her masterpiece, propped on the kitchen windowsill on its way to the library. She had dissected this owl-pellet alone and unaided, cleaned and sterilised all the delicate bits she had retrieved from it, and glued them in place on the black card which showed them off so clearly. Kemp said it was now a valuable record of what a hawk owl ate in June in a Swiss forest.

I'm useful enough to him, so why doesn't he. . .? Sally's thoughts came to a halt there, as they always did, and she snuffed up the appetising savour of the cheese she was slicing. Maybe she was just hungry.

You were meant to toast the end of this long block in the farmhouse stove, then cut it off and eat it. Modern Swiss, she'd been fascinated to learn, fitted slices into tiny steel shovels, and toasted them by electricity.

'And, this evening, so will we.' She took the cheese-toaster into the new room, and set it on the kitchen table she had insisted on having in here. 'Swiss food, for a Swiss castle.'

She had to admit Kemp was right about this table. It did look absurd, stuck here in a stately window embrasure with the breathtaking sweep of valley and mountains beyond it. The ever-bluer lines of horizon and distant, cloudy peaks made it seem squarer than ever on its little legs with its little chairs snuggled up to it.

'Like corgis in the royal apartments,' Kemp had jeered after he'd carried them there for her this morning. 'Mother and pups.'

'It'll do until we find something better,' Sally had replied with dignity. 'At least we'll be able to enjoy the view at supper, and celebrate this room's being finished.'

Kemp still wasn't back with the post, so she went to wait for him in the study. Not that she could relax, even curled like this into his enormous chair. Her gaze kept straying to the window, and then if she didn't wake up she'd find she was staring across the courtyard, under the stone arch, away to the sun-speckled track that wound out of her view into gold-green forest.

I want him back, she realised. I want him to rampage the way he used to, and then I want him to. . .

But she couldn't put that into words, not even to herself. It was bad enough the way she dreamt of it, sleeping and waking.

Here he was at last. From the distance, striding along in those seven-league boots, he seemed exactly the same fiery spirit she'd first known, and. . .yes, and fallen in love with. Only as he joined her in the study did she wonder, as she'd wondered so often in the last two months, if that Kemp had gone forever.

'One for you.' He held it out to her, carefully not looking at the large brown envelope.

She thanked him, and opened it quickly. She wasn't much interested in it, but it helped take her mind off the gingerly way he was lowering himself to the bed which was their only other seat. She'd done her best to conceal its real use, covering it with the multi-coloured crochet blanket from the farmhouse and arranging his duvet and pillows as daytime backrests. But he never relaxed enough to lean back, and he still treated the bed as if it might explode under him.

'Won't you have this chair?' she asked as she always did. 'You'd be far more comfortable.'

'I wouldn't. Yesterday, when you sat here, you ended up lying down full length.'

'I took my shoes off first.'

'Exactly.' Kemp looked down at her feet in their delicate high-heeled sandals, and froze. 'You've. . .you've painted your toenails!'

'It's not a crime.' Sally stretched her bare brown legs before her to admire her pearl-tipped toes. 'I did it last night. Seeing that I meant to dress up a little, for once.'

'Very pretty.' But he no longer looked at her feet. 'Very. . .' his glance went from one to the other of her tanned arms, paused briefly at her cool V-neck, skipped to her waist, and settled at last on the fullness of her skirt '. . .pretty,' he finished gruffly. 'Aren't you going to read your letter?'

She nodded, and finished opening the envelope. Most of the contents seemed to be pages torn from a colour supplement, along with its cover, where titles jostled each other, and one in particular caught her eye.

'THE WAR BETWEEN THE FISHERS'.

She went on to the next pages, letting the cover picture fall to her lap.

'Isn't that Walsh and his silly little Tara?' queried Kemp.

'Not *his*.' Interested in the story, Sally settled to read the first page of the article and left the next dangling from her fingers.

'Let's see.' Kemp leant across to take it.

She stiffened, and stopped reading. Even through the cotton of her dress, the tiny brush of his knuckles against her thighs had left her helpless. She could feel it spreading through her like the beams of a sensual lighthouse.

And he hadn't even noticed. He was on his feet now, intent only on the text of the page she hadn't reached yet.

'What the hell is this?'

'I don't know.' She drew a long, hissing breath. 'But I'd guess. . .'

She had to stop and struggle for self-control. That was better. Not good—she still felt like wax melting in the sun—but better.

'Give it here,' She tried to take the page back. 'I haven't reached that bit yet.'

'As if you didn't know what's in it!' Kemp waved the page at her. '"Kingfisher's publicity continues with Limelight's Sally Benedict, who tips a mean cup of coffee,"' he read aloud, '"though director Mark Walsh seems to have forgiven all. . ."'

'Let me see!'

She stood up and grabbed for the pages, but that brought her much too close to him. She couldn't breathe, couldn't see, couldn't think in this hammering, melting, whirling closeness.

'This whole damn section's about you two.' Kemp pointed to another photo, and read its caption aloud. '". . .enjoying a cosy supper in spite of rumours that she's the new. . ."' he stopped in appalled disbelief, then continued on a questioning note '". . .the new love of Kemp Whittaker. . ."?'

If only it were true! But he was showing all too clearly how he felt about it. He didn't want to know, couldn't see her yearning, had already gone on to the next picture.

'I see you got together right at the airport,' he added.

'We didn't—that was his idiot friend's idea of a joke. He had us both called urgently to the desk. . .' Sally trailed off, hating to be reminded of Mark's sullen glare, the untreated coffee stains darkening his light suit, the cackling Barnes and his camera. 'Neither of us knew he was taking the picture.'

'But you've put it to good use.'

'*Who* has?' she floundered, unable to believe her ears.

'All publicity's good publicity,' Kemp reminded her through his teeth. '". . .straight after the coffee-pouring incident. . .showing the kind of hate that's really love. . ."' His eyes moved to the foot of the page. 'Bloody hell!'

Sally craned to see what had caused this new outburst. The stock shot of himself was superimposed on another of the castle, as if he were standing in front of it. So Tara had faked an endorsement for herself, and then sold it on scandal. The last picture was a gossip-column shot of Sally and Mark cheek to cheek, her naked arms round his neck, her near-naked bosom pressed to his dinner jacket, her short-skirted thighs close to his. The text hinted at a love triangle which might develop further in the autumn hunting season, when clients of Queenfisher. . . Et cetera.

'So this is what it's been about!' Kemp tore the article in two and dashed it to the floor. 'You damned little two-timer!'

Sally quailed before his anger. 'You can't really think I——'

'Don't come the innocent—you're not clever enough—*Sal*!' He almost spat the hated nickname. 'I saw how you were just now!'

'You d-did?'

'Has this come out earlier than you planned?' He gestured down at the torn pages. 'Did you expect to be well clear before it broke? Is that why you couldn't look me in the face?'

'So you did notice. . .'

She stopped, and swallowed hard. How could she ever tell him the real reason for her blushes? How did you say, It's because I want you to make love to me? Maybe some women could, but she wasn't one of them. And because she couldn't, he was taking her confusion for guilt.

'Have you earned yourself promotion, you little

cheat?' He grabbed her shoulders. 'Are you going back to be a bigger and better cheat, like your boyfriend?'

'You're hurting. . .'

Sally twisted one way and another in his cruel grip. It eased at once, and somehow his restraint was more than she could bear. She shook her head, wanting to hide from the blurry, unmanageable sight of him, fighting the tears that welled behind her closed eyelids. But they wouldn't be kept in; she could feel them escaping and running down her cheeks.

And here was his finger, stroking them lightly away though he tried to stay tough. 'You women and your weeping!'

She sniffed angrily. 'It never does any good.'

'I wouldn't say that.' One of his hands had stolen to the nape of her neck while the other played with her cheek, settled under her chin, forced it up. 'Open your eyes.'

She obeyed, nerving herself to meet that diamond-hard gaze. It wasn't hard now but deep, dark, compelling.

'I thought so. Crying makes your eyes the colour of the forest after rain.'

His mouth came down on hers, and at last she knew what to do. She only needed to open her lips like this, strain to him like this, and the rest was easy. The whole universe was with them, rushing to circle and bind them, closing them in a ring of sun and moon and stars, earth and air and fire, fire; above all, fire.

By the time Kemp had released her, the fire was raging within her. She helped him loosen her dress with burning fingers, let him push it down from her burning breasts, moved her burning hips for him so he could slide it to the ground along with the little else she wore.

'If only you weren't so beautiful. . .' And he knelt to

her womanhood, hands and lips sparking new fire wherever they touched.

'May I, Kemp?' she pleaded when she could bear it no longer. 'May I?'

And then came a brief chill of apartness while he tore the shirt from his broad, tanned, dark-haired chest, the denim from his narrow hips. Her breasts rose, ever more taut from the mere heat of his gaze, but he didn't move to touch her again, only stood before her in the superb nakedness she had once feared and rejected and was now ready to treasure. She dropped to her knees as he had shown her how to do, and presently he lifted her in his arms, set her on the bed which was, after all, so gloriously a bed, and took her by storm.

And finished the journey to fulfilment without her.

At least he was still close, she consoled herself. But when he had done, and recovered, he got up and left her without a word.

She lay listening to the water running in the bathroom, and hated him. Then he returned, and moved to the bed, and lifted her in his arms again, and it was going to be all right—wasn't it?

It wasn't. He only set her on her feet, pinned her with one arm to his side, and pulled the blanket from under where they had been lying.

And that turned out to be it. When he had wrapped her up, covered her right up to the chin, he grabbed the rolled duvet for himself and retreated to the chair, leaving her to sink, wool-draped and miserably alone, to the bed.

'So that's what it's all about.' Her own voice dropped leaden in her ears. 'And to think I might have a baby now!'

'What?' His top half shot up like a sea-god from the

foam of duvet. 'I know you weren't on the Pill when we first met, but you're surely taking it now.'

'Of course not! Why should I?'

'You can't want a little Walsh?' He scowled at her concealing pyramid of blanket. 'If you're aiming to get pregnant by him so he'll marry you, think again. That's not his——'

'I can't believe I'm hearing this!' She straightened in outrage, not caring if the blanket stayed round her or not. 'Do you honestly still think I——'

'I don't have to think it.' His bare foot emerged from the lower end of the duvet to stir the torn pages. 'It's all there.'

'It is *not*!' Reckless with fury, Sally rose from her shell of blanket and knelt to scramble through the little pile of papers until she came to the picture of herself and Mark cheek to cheek. 'See that?' she held it up to him.

Kemp turned his head away. 'I've seen enough.'

'You'll look at it, or I'll. . .'

She'd what? She was suddenly overwhelmed with her own helplessness, alone and naked before a man who believed the worst of her. A man who had knelt to her, as she had to him, and yet now he had brought her to her knees again, and the dream was ending in nightmare.

'I w-worshipped you, the way you promise when you marry,' she stammered, hardly knowing what she was saying. 'W-with my body I thee w-worship. . .' But she couldn't go on.

'For heaven's sake don't cry, woman!'

'I'm not.' Still clutching the picture, Sally put her arm over her eyes to shield herself. 'Or if I am, it's p-private.'

'Very private, with you like that!' His exasperation

pierced the swimming darkness behind her closed lids. 'Surely you know by now what it makes me. . .' He ground to a stop, and she felt the picture snatched from her grasp. 'Give it here, then. Though what the hell it's supposed to prove. . .'

'They took it at the Silk launching, back in March.' She lowered her arm and stared earnestly at him, a sob caught in her throat. 'Do you really think I could l-let him anywhere near me, once I'd met *you*?'

'I don't know what I think any more. Right now. . .' his gaze swept from her tear-wet face and down over her body, before he dragged it away and fixed it somewhere above her left shoulder. . .'thinking isn't what I'm doing.'

'But you must!' Sally sprang up to stand by him and point to her pictured dress. 'Don't you recognise that? It's the one you tore apart the night of Dr Elise's birthday.'

'You mended it?' Kemp frowned down at the flaunting red silk.

'It's in the farmhouse duster cupboard,' she told him.

'Or bought another like it?'

'As if I would! I d-don't wear that kind of thing any more.'

'N-no,' he admitted reluctantly, with a glance at the modest summer dress crumpled among the debris on the floor. 'What about the cosy supper, then? Is that an old picture too?'

'It's from the only time he ever took me out,' she said.

'I. . .see.' It came out heavy, pensive, the braking and slow redirecting of a whole, headlong set of ideas. 'So who's dredged up this lot, if it wasn't you?'

'Tara, of course. This is about the rivalry between her firm and Mark's. She said she'd smash him. . .'

'Is that why she's sent you this lot?'

'She didn't; it's from my mother.' Sally crossed to the couch for the envelope, heedless of his quickened breathing. 'See?' She brought it over to show him the Devon postmark.

'It's. . .' Kemp stared rigidly at the envelope, not making the least move that might bring her unconcealed body into his field of vision. 'It's addressed by computer.'

'They have one for the farm. Mum uses it a lot—haven't you noticed?' Sally stooped to pick up the typed letter from where it had fluttered close to his foot, which hastily withdrew to its sheltering duvet. 'I thought so.' She read it quickly through. 'She says somebody in the village gave her these, and what's it all about?'

'Let's see.' He accepted it with a clumsiness utterly unlike him. 'Oh, good lord!' He handed it back, head turned away from her. 'I'd say sorry, if it weren't so pathetically not enough.'

'There's nothing pathetic about you, Kemp Whittaker.' She accepted the letter, and put it back in the envelope. 'Hateful, sometimes. . .'

'Like just now?' His voice was hollow, humbled.

'You said some loathsome things——'

'I'll never be able to forgive myself. Will you ever——?'

'But the worst of all was when you went away and left me.'

'It was meant to be.' He turned to her, trying to explain. 'I thought. . . I mean, I wanted to. . .'

He trailed off, eyes half closed, nostrils dilated. 'Do me a favour, Sally,' he hissed in desperation. 'Cover yourself. Not with that!' Some of his force returned as she picked up her dress. 'That's nearly as bad!'

'It isn't!'

Indignant and bewildered, Sally paused with the dress in front of her. His hand shot out as if to grasp it, then clenched and dropped once more to the arm of his chair.

'You see?' The tortured growl came from deep in his throat. 'If you start putting that on, I doubt if I'd let you finish.'

'Oh.' She looked down at herself, and back at him. 'You mean, even after what we did just now you——?'

'Just don't stand there, woman!' He flung aside the duvet, shot past her to the blanket, and covered her with it for the second time. 'Now get away from me!'

She stayed where she was, round-eyed from her brief glimpse of his nakedness. 'Are you always like that?'

'Of course not!' He had the duvet once more safely over himself. 'I mean—well, only since I met you.'

'What about with Tara?'

'Mind your own business!'

'Tell me, or I'll. . .' She paused, still at a loss for any meaningful threat, then grasped the edges of her blanket with a slow smile. 'Or I'll take this off.'

'Sit down, then,' he broke in hurriedly. 'I'm not saying another word till you're over there where I can't reach you.'

She obeyed. 'Why did you go off with her at the party?'

'Because I can't be civil to Walsh.'

'You left *me* with him,' Sally pointed out.

'I thought that was what you wanted. Have you forgotten how set you were on that wretched job?'

'I was, wasn't I?' she marvelled at her old, blind self. 'But you don't get me off Tara that easily, Kemp Whittaker. When you turned her down——'

'You know about that, do you?'

'Didn't you fancy her at all? Not the least little bit?'

'Of course I did. A little. Enough,' he conceded angrily. 'I'm a man like any other. But she'd have been a. . .' he shrugged, glossy brown shoulders rippling '. . .a Sally substitute, and I don't use women in that way. Though I don't expect you to believe me now.'

'A S-Sally s-substitute. What a tongue-twister!' she joked feebly through her own racing pulses.

'After two whole months of holding back.' Kemp thumped the arm of his chair in despair. 'Two months of showing I could keep my temper like anybody else. . .'

'So that's what the trouble was!'

'Trouble? It's been murder.' He raised his eyes to hers. 'I only stuck it because I had to prove it wouldn't be a raving, stamping maniac you'd be marrying. . .'

'I'd be what?' She sat erect within her blanket.

'And now I've flipped, and raped you, I'll never——'

'You've *what*?' she interrupted, astonished by his view of what had happened. 'I rather thought I—er—helped—a little.'

'You weren't with me, though, were you? I didn't mean you to be.'

'You kissed me. . .'

'I had to,' he admitted, as if to a weakness. 'But I still meant to keep it wham, bam, thank you, ma'am.'

'Kemp!' she exclaimed, half amused, half appalled. 'Is that how men talk about these things?'

'Sometimes. When they feel like I was feeling then. Only,' his voice broke, 'you're so be tiful when you're naked, I had to. . .to worship.'

'Me too,' she agreed softly. 'With my body, I thee. . .'

'I didn't understand that, Sally,' he explained, shamefaced. 'I thought Walsh must have taught you. . . Oh, lord!' He dropped his forehead on his clenched fist. 'After the way I've dreamed of our first time together! It was going to be a memory we'd treasure all our lives.'

'I don't know about that,' Sally objected doubtfully. 'It hurt, a little.'

'It needn't have. Or maybe just a little,' Kemp acknowledged with his usual truthfulness. 'But I needn't have treated you the way I did. . .' He glanced in her direction and came to an abrupt, fascinated pause.

'Would you mind reorganising that blanket?' he asked, hoarse but polite as a fellow passenger in a railway carriage. 'One of the openwork bits is right over——'

'Is it?'

Sally looked down, then deliberately pulled the blanket tight over that breast. The wool was deep blue at this point, she noted with satisfaction. Just right for setting off the pink that peeped between the woven, patterned shells.

'It makes me think of an. . .' Kemp licked his lips, and tried again. 'Of an. . .inquisitive. . .baby mouse.'

'Is that a compliment?' She surveyed him through lowered lashes.

'I. . .like. . .mice.'

Then he had left his protecting duvet, and was by her on the bed. Excitement rearing from his loins, he took the questing nipple between finger and thumb, his other hand teasing its twin beneath the strands of wool until it, too, found an opening, and nuzzled into his fingers.

'Is it love, Kemp?' Sally gasped, the sensual beams

raying again through her blood. 'Love, and marriage, and children?'

'You'll still have me?' he murmured as if he couldn't believe his luck.

'Try me.'

She never did know what happened to the blanket. They found it crumpled on the floor, but that was much later. By then it had all happened, his hands on her body, his lips on her breasts until the pleasure burnt and demanded within her, and she begged him to stop, to go on, to leave her, to take her. And still he wouldn't, but instead kissed her belly, filled her navel with his tongue and traced a pattern of kisses from one of her hips to the other, from one of her thighs to the other, circling ever closer to the place where his kisses were welcome but not enough, not enough, never, never enough. Only when she beat her fists on his shoulders did he stretch himself over her and let her fire consume his, let the blaze toss them together into some world beyond time and space which presently dissolved in rhythmic floods of ecstasy.

'So *that's* what it's all about,' she murmured at last, close to his shoulder. 'Now I can *understand* how women get babies even when they don't mean to.'

Kemp kissed her hair. 'How you keep on about babies!'

'Well, I like them. They're better than mice.'

'Nothing could be better than these mice.' He cupped her breasts, and kissed each newly stirring tip.

'Oh, my darling!' She clung to him. 'If we carry on like this, there'll be lots and lots of babies.' She drew back to look into the blue-grey eyes, resisting the new gleam which was lighting them. 'Is it all right, my having lots of babies?'

'Little Sallys.' He tried out the idea. 'I'd like that.'

'There'll be little Kemps too.'

'As long as they're all little Whittakers.' He filled her hand with a harvest of small, hard kisses. 'I promise I'll make them be good.' He stroked her belly. 'Good as——What was that?' He unfolded from her and put his feet to the floor so he could set his ear against her stomach. 'Isn't it a bit early for those babies to be talking back to us?'

'Fool!' Sally giggled. 'Is it any wonder my tummy rumbles, after all the exercise we've had today?' She pushed him away so she could stand up. 'We're long overdue for supper.'

'Ah, yes, supper.' Kemp followed her with his eyes as she rescued her dress. 'I've been meaning to talk to you about that.'

'Talk away. Is it all right if I put this on now?'

'Temporarily.' He found his shirt, and shrugged into it. 'We have to make ourselves decent, to get down to the farmhouse.'

'Are we going to live there?' She smoothed the creases from his shirt.

'Until we've got a bedroom fixed here. Longer, if you want. Careful!' He finished buttoning the shirt, and picked up his jeans. 'I need to keep these on.'

'You certainly do.' She obediently left him alone, and went to the big chair where, walled by the discarded duvet, she put on her sandals. 'We really must eat.'

'We must. Listen, Sally.' Covered as far as his still bare feet, Kemp sank solemnly to the bed opposite her. 'Frau Hüber's left a casserole in the farmhouse oven.'

'Why, Kemp Whittaker!' Her sandal only half

buckled, Sally looked up at him in reproof. 'You never meant to eat in the new room at all!'

'Not till it stops reeking of paint.'

'And what about my *raclette*?'

'It'll do for a snack some time. Today,' he leant forward to impress her with the importance of what he was saying, 'after hours in the forest with nothing but a couple of rolls. . .'

'Of various kinds.' She rose to sit on his lap, put her arms round his neck, bury her fingers in his dear wild hair and feel his dear rough cheek against hers. 'There goes *your* tum.'

'Exactly. A man needs more than a bit of melted cheese.' He held her close. 'You'd better learn that, Sally Benedict-soon-to-be-Whittaker.' He kissed her ear. 'You forgive me, then?'

'On one condition.'

'Name it.'

'That you propose to me properly. What are you doing?' as she felt herself swung through the air and dumped in the great chair. 'You can't keep throwing ladies around like this, Kemp Whittaker!'

'Not ladies.' He knelt at her feet. 'Only you.' He leant forward to span her waist with his hands. 'Only you, my darling. . . Wait a minute, you're distracting me.'

He moved back to his earlier position, one knee before him, back straight, eyes tender.

'I love you, Sally Benedict. Will you marry me?'

Next month's Romances

Each month, you can choose from a world of variety in romance with Mills & Boon. These are the new titles to look out for next month.

NO GENTLE SEDUCTION Helen Bianchin

THE FINAL TOUCH Betty Neels

TWIN TORMENT Sally Wentworth

JUNGLE ENCHANTMENT Patricia Wilson

DANCE FOR A STRANGER Susanne McCarthy

THE DARK SIDE OF DESIRE Michelle Reid

WITH STRINGS ATTACHED Vanessa Grant

BARRIER TO LOVE Rosemary Hammond

FAR FROM OVER Valerie Parv

HIJACKED HONEYMOON Eleanor Rees

DREAMS ARE FOR LIVING Natalie Fox

PLAYING BY THE RULES Kathryn Ross

ONCE A CHEAT Jane Donnelly

HEART IN FLAMES Sally Cook

KINGFISHER MORNING Charlotte Lamb

STARSIGN

STING IN THE TAIL Annabel Murray

Available from Boots, Martins, John Menzies, W.H. Smith, Woolworths and other paperback stockists.

Also available from Mills and Boon Reader Service, P.O. Box 236, Thornton Road, Croydon, Surrey CR9 3RU.